# A Therapy of Camels

# A Therapy of Camels

## William Oliphant

Chapman Publications
1995

Published by
Chapman
4 Broughton Place
Edinburgh EH1 3RX
Scotland

A catalogue record for this volume is
available from the British Library.
ISBN 0-906772-49-4

Chapman New Writing Series
Editor Joy Hendry
ISSN 0953-5306

Some of these stories have previously appeared in
*Chapman, The Jewish Quarterly, Scottish Stories from MacGregor's
Gathering* and *West Coast Magazine*

Designed & typeset by Peter Cudmore
Cover design: Fred Crayk
Photo (back cover): W.H. Mills

Printed by
Mayfair Printers
Print House
Commercial Road
Hendon
Sunderland

# Contents

# Bearsden Bagatelle

## Part one: Fuhll Bladders in the Paurley

The news story transportit me back owr fifty year tae
Parliamentary Road it the end i the twinties: "The Paurley" i ma
furst decade.

The Paurley runs (ur ran) fae Castle Street tae Sauchiehall
Street which, although east n west, tae us wis aywis up n doon.
The rid tramcaurs gaun up wur headit fur Bishopbriggs ur
Millerston, the blue fur Alexandra Park. Oan the doon line, the
rid wur fur Merrylee, Giffnock n Rouken Glen, n the blue,
Kirklee ur Scotstoun. Thae names fae the destination boards wur
aw familiar tae us long afore we iver saw thum is places, ur even
knew whoar they wur.

The caurs thursels, sweein, clangin, thundern past oor
coarner, wur essential features i the lanscape. It wis jist is if they
hid occurred in Nature tae fillfu' the uses we pit thum tae. They
produced the coloured doackets we collectit is substitutes fur
cigarette cairds, they oaffered free hurls atween stoaps if ye wur
brave enough tae hing oanty the brass haunrail whin the
conductor wis up the sterrs, n they wur a source a pleesure n
terror if· ye hud tae jump aff it speed. Aw kindsa explosive
compounds wur detonatit bi thur iron wheels, beer boatle taps
wur flattened bi thum, n the steel rails they ran oan wur
convenient geometrical divisions in the road way fur competitive
purposes.

The gemme ah huv in mind hud nae pipe-baun waarm-up lik
a Hampden afferr, bit it startit oaf wi a helluva loata runnin in in
oota hooses fur drinks a watter. Minny a maw musta bin hert-
roastit long afore the skaillin fuhllness a bladder, a precondition
a entry, wis achieved.

Ah'm no talkin aboot kids jist peein in the street, even peein
well oot intae the street. Kerbside urination hud bin elevatit tae
the level a high art. We'd perfectit a technique thit involved

7

fuhllin the space atween phallus n foreskin tae the latter swelt lik a fitba bladder, then releasin the pressure a finger n thumb so thit an atomised spurt hurtled itsel ootwards acroass the road. Wi due attention peyed tae trajectory n wind velocity phenomenal ranges wur achieved. We could aw reach beyond the saicant caur rail, n Wattie Houston, hauder i the championship, hud, wi a wee bit help fae a foaleyin wind thit swirled doon Black Street it the psychological moment, passed the thurd.

In the very nature a things we contendit is individuals, the wans thit did contend, that is. Francis Nimmo, ah mind, wis a non-starter because id bin circumcised is a wean. It wisnae thi kinna gemme thit separatit us intae teams, cock ur hen, spit ur dry. No lik fitba wherr we identified wi Ranger ur Celtic dependin oan whether we went tae Kennedy Street School ur St Mungo Primary. It the kerb each man stuck oot oan is ain, n although the spectaturs wur partisan, they wurnae sectarian.

Alastair Finn, wee hard man i the group a unemployed youths thit hung aboot the coarner, made a book whiniver we competit. He could calculate odds wi a facility thit nane i the Maths teachers in St Mungo's hud iver suspected, n bets wur laid, won n loast in hauf Woodbines. Excitement oaften ran high. Bladders wur fuhlled n empied, fuhlled again n empied, n oan a number i occasions weemin staunin oan the platforms a eastbound caurs hud thur stoackins sprayed bi mistimed ur over-enthusiastic ejections.

Ah suppose the Polis wid ultimately huv pit a stoap tae wur innocent fun – that's whut Polis wur fur in thae days – bit McTaggart beat thum tae it. McTaggart wis a bit bigger n aulder thin the rest i us. He wis kinna new tae the district, so nane i us kent much aboot um, n he hudny much tae say fur issel. Whin we lined the kerbside n committit wursels tae the excitement i the match, he usually stood tae the wan side n looked inscrutably oan.

Only wance did he cheynge this pattern. It wis durin a lull in the proceedins, while we restit n refuelled, he wis seen tae step tae the pavement's edge, unbutton is fly, n send an unbroken yellow stream in a great parabolic curve oot n beyond the fourth rail. Tae this day ah cin see the scunner oan Wattie Houston's face as he watched is hard-won record sae nonchalantly shattered.

We niver played the gemme again. McTaggart, it turned oot,

wis ninety per cent foreskin. Ye canny compete wi deformity.

It wis in a copy i the Westerton n Bearsden Chronicle ah picked up accidentally thit ah saw the news story:

> A 65-year-old company director from Bearsden was fined £10 when he appeared at the Burgh Court on Monday. Walter Templeton Houston admitted charges of breach of the peace and indecent exposure outside his luxury flat in Grove Park. The Burgh Prosecutor told the Court that two nights earlier a police constable on patrol had seen the accused urinating from a fourth-floor balcony. Houston was arrested and charged at Bearsden Police Station. Houston's agent said, "My client is normally a moderate man, but he had taken drink that evening, and did not know what he was doing. He is extremely sorry and wishes to assure the Court that such an incident will not reoccur." Earlier the Prosecution told the Court that Houston was heard to shout, "How's that for the car rails?"

Ah read it through twice. It jist hud tae be the same Wattie Houston. Company director? Luxury flat? Wattie hud done well fur issel. Ah wunnered who ur whut hud driven um tae flaunt is origins oan is luxury balcony, whut conflict hud caused um tae regress aw the wey back tae the thurd caur rail oan Paurley Road. It wid've bin ridiculous fur me tae phone um – he wis jist a face na foreskin fae the mists i ma childhood – bit in ma imagination ah wis diallin is number.

"Mr Houston? As representative of the Paurley Pissers of the Past Association, ah regret tae hufty inform you thit yur recent record attempt his bin declerred null n void because a the advantage a elevation..."

Regression cin be infectious. That night in the bathroom, whin ah wis gettin ready fur ma bed, ah hud a sudden impulse tae try ma haun it the auld gemme. Mibby it wis lack a practice, mibby even sheer physical development, thit explains ma disastrous failure. Is ah mopped up the lavvy flerr, ah reflected philosophically oan how minny things git loast in the years atween.

9

## Part two: Visiting Marian

Easy Wattie, easy. Gently now. There's a definite tendency to stagger and a definite tendency to spray on the labial plosives – oh God bless the labial plosives! – and a definite tendency to weep whisky tears into the beer, only there's no beer here.

Steady, Wattie. There's a pillar on the porch to lean against – Corporation Corinthian! – and a green door set in the faced brick – Council-House-Baronial! – and a cute little perspex rectangle with the name in black letters on silver paper:

M. MCGONAGLE

A mick! Slum Irish and Fenian. What the hell's she doing tied to one of those? There's a chromium bell push and the nipped sound of strangled chimes, plink-plonk like a double hernia, and Marian at the door, fat, dark, smiling and ready, and the smile fading a little when her notice is arrested by the sound and the stagger and the smell of the whisky.

Humble apologies to dear, sweet, accommodating Marian. She has seen you that way and yon, up and down, bird's eye and worm's eye, but never cut, never the need, and never now if it wasn't for the court this morning and that whining bastard of a lawyer and the indecent exposure. And how is she? And the six steps and stairs McGonagles that have all come out of her, and the big horny McGonagle who gives her babies and Christ knows what pleasures, except that they're not enough since she'll take all you can give her for pure enjoyment. And it's not lost what a friend gets. And a change is as good as a rest. And what nobody knows doesn't do them any harm.

Humble apologies to mollify Marian and the smile is back, though the withdrawn look in the eye is the Saturday-night calculation of dates. Don't wave your menstrual calendar at me, Marian. That's for drunken Irish micks. This is me, Wattie, cock with a Protestant conscience, user of contraceptive devices on every conceivable occasion, purveyor of many pleasures and never an anxious moment despite your manifest predilection for pregnancy. And how's that for labial plosives?

Now straight for the fire, Wattie, for it's raining misery outside, and sit at the right hand with Marian opposite so you can look up her skirt. Drink tea, the thick tarry brew which seems always to be on the gas, and eat a roll, two rolls, with spam. And talk! Talk the kind of talk you would never talk sober. You can tell

10

her she is beautiful and she will never believe you mean it because of the whisky. Although in a way it's perfectly true. Dear good old Marian with her belly muscles slackening and her great breasts beginning to sag, with the smur of blue hair under her oxters, the massive rotundity of hips and the shaggy ridge of pelvis. Dear, fat, sweet Marian, the only woman you know whose nakedness doesn't proclaim, "This is my body!" but quietly, "This is me!" Self-acceptance, and it makes her acceptable, and beautiful.

More tea, Wattie. More of the hot, sweet, tarry scald. Tea is an aphrodisiac! Who needs it with the view up her skirt and the way the weight of the teapot flexes her bare arm and modifies the line of her breast? Hot and sweet, feed it to the patient for shock.

Admit to the shock, Wattie. Admit to the shock of appearing in that place for that reason, for all the arrogant air, for all the sophisticated nonchalance. The man-about-town caught short in public. And the bland, blond advocate full of the confident courage of his own lies, and the world-bleary, idiot-chinned naïve sadist on the bench, and the smell of terror from the drunk drivers waiting on the back row, and the smirk and the sniff and the pencil-chewing Pitmans of the Westerton and Bearsden Chronicle.

Admit to the shock, Wattie, and to the sudden up-rearing vision of Agnes prostrate, mortally mortified, riding her sofa in a shipwreck of shame, a peaky motionless figure on an overstuffed raft adrift on a neutral, opinionless sea of wall-to-wall. And that's what you wanted, Wattie, at the time. But it was the drink, and you're not used to the drink, and here we are again.

No, don't move, Marian!

Her movements are too provocative, and you still have all those words first before you lose your senses in her provocative movements, all those words the whisky has smoked up into the top of your brain, and they'll take your skull off like a Cherokee in a hurry if you don't open your mouth and let the words tumble out on to the floor. Or on to somebody's lap, on to Marian's lap, because it is so voluminous. If you can bury your face in such a lap and forget your fever, you can bury your words in it and maybe turn their edge.

Words! Words! Words! There was a time, Wattie, when you wouldn't have had the words, but you've read a book or two since then. Walter T Houston, Company Director, has the words, a plethora of words. Words are instruments that torture images.

"Agnes!" you would say in a tender moment. "You're still the best feel in Bearsden." And that would stiffen her. Yet the words were not what you meant, and she would have known that had she been listening to you with her guts instead of her brain. Well of course you've felt your way around Bearsden. Middle-class arses, and they're not all cold, not by a long chalk, but they're all so bloody neurotic. Sex doesn't so much function as break out like a rash. It's a disease, an abnormality. For a couple to lie down together and have a straightforward enjoyable shag is some kind of perversion. Animal instincts! As if there were any other kind.

And Wattie! You don't really understand what it's all about, do you? What is it with Agnes and her middle-class cronies, the vested virgins of the west? Middle-class is the wrong term. You use it just as a derogatory noise, a label of contempt remembered from childhood contact with dole queues, hunger marches, slogans chalked on tenement walls, and fried bread. Bourgeois is just as meaningless, although it has more of a growl to it.

What is it then? It's not class, and it's not politics, and it's not long noses nor the West-end affectations of voice and syntax. But it has something to do with wall-to-wall carpeting and drinks on the sideboard and the abstract over the mantelpiece. And it has something to do with Daddy's money, even though, for Christ's sake, Daddy started life as a common bricky, and it has to do with 'A Liberal View of Sexual Morality' with as little actual nookie as her man will put up with, and maybe – you don't know – but just maybe there is some guilt in it. Maybe there is guilt for a morganatic marriage, guilt for the working-class bun in the middle-class oven, guilt for being Wattie's feel, the best in Bearsden, a two-orgasm woman caught in the mixter-maxter tradition of 'The Liberal View' on the one hand, and strict Calvinistic continence on the other.

All right, Agnes, all right! None of that is fair. When we come down to it, it's all a matter of humiliation:

Wattie humiliated. The majesty of the Law triumphant.

Agnes humiliated. Her shame sprayed from her luxury balcony into her luxury courtyard within sight and sound of her luxury friends.

And the two humiliations have still to meet and be reconciled, and may the good Lord preserve us all.

12

So move over, Marion McGonagle, who was Marian
MacLelland, a hundred fecund years ago, and move over, Wattie,
to bury your face in the plump mother-breasts that cushion all
the shocks, and your hands on the white, warm thighs, and the
gall slowly draining away. And she'll not let you sleep too long,
Wattie, if you should sleep, for the steps and stairs McGonagles
will all be in from school at four.


## Part three: Agnes on Stockie Muir

What she felt around her here was the sky and the cleansing
Stockie Muir wind. The tussocky grass was wet from he
morning's rain, but her boots were proof against it, and she was
well clad, and knew how to avoid the real bogs. It was clear and
bright now and Queen's View was glorious.

She had not come for the glories of the view or, indeed, for
the enfolding sky or the antiseptic wind. She came because
Bearsden stifled her. There were too many familiar faces in and
around the shops, the hush of the library deafened her, and the
church was merely the church; a place for gossip and flower-
arranging, for cups of tea and sympathetic friends who said they
were sorry and enjoyed their own compassion.

She could have gone to the Burgh Court this morning and
gloated. But she refrained. The games they play there are
inappropriate and irrelevant. Already, in her made-up mind, she
had assembled all the facts and decided that they too were
irrelevant. She had not come to the Muir to think. The thinking
was done. She had come to square her shoulders, to straighten
a spiritual stoop that had, she became aware, been developing
for years.

Away to her left she saw the Whangie, that strange formation
of rock, cliff and chasm so beloved by the nursery climbers of
Glasgow. She half-remembered the legend connecting it to the
Devil's hoofprint, one step taken between the Islands and
Edinburgh, before his heel-swerve south to fields more fertile for
his purposes. She smiled at the thought of Auld Nick taken short
on Stockie Muir and turning his great, black, pointed pintle to lay
down Loch Lomond and shake off the drips to form the
reservoirs between here and Dumbarton.

There was no smell now of Satanic influence. She stood in a

small wet wilderness and, surrounded by it, experienced a sense of liberation. She was liberated by the sky and the wind, by rock and bog, by a teasing glimpse of loch and the view of mountains to the north. She was freed by the thought of Old Horny so spectacularly relieving himself. She remained perfectly still for a long time and breathed in what she took to be the spirit of the Muir. Then, as she turned and began to retrace her steps towards the car park, she consciously shed the burden of the Little-Boy-Lost, and watched, with some astonishment at her own detachment, a fading vision of a last, petulant flash of phallic pride, and a pathetic yellow stream splashing ineptly into the front lawn.

# A Round of Letterboxes

Billy rose at five, slipping quietly out of the hole-in-the-wall bed so as not to disturb his younger brother. He made a quick breakfast of tea and fried bread, and hurried down the worn stone stairs into the wet, gas-lit, magic, October streets. It wasn't a real job, delivering papers morning and evening for Mr. Inglis, Newsagent, at five shillings a week, but he was only just left school, only a month past his fourteenth birthday, and this gave him time to look around.

He had already learned a few things. You could feel important, getting up before even your mother, making your own breakfast; handing in, on a Friday, enough to pay half the rent. He had discovered, too, how different the morning darkness was from night. He liked the feel of this dark city before it woke, the hush, the hint of mystery about the quiet streets that made them appear off-focus and slightly dangerous. And he had discovered the thrill of black and bright red against the yellow-green of gaslight. Her hair was black, and she wore a red cardigan, and the gaslight was behind her as he handed in her paper, and she smiled at him, and said 'thank you', and closed the door quite slowly.

He walked down Glebe Street whistling under his breath, and turned into Kennedy Street at the school. The Infant's Playground, full of familiar corners, was transformed into a haunted courtyard by unfamiliar shadows. The pend that led to Howard's stable was quiet, and smelt of straw and dung. In the distance across the street he saw the glow of the forge through the back window of the smithy.

Wattie Houston was waiting for him at the corner of Black Street. Even at that hour he had an old tennis ball and was playing 'wee headers' against the door of the church hall. When he saw Billy approach, he tossed the ball towards him and dashed off down the street.

"Right Billy! The wing! The wing!"

Billy killed the ball with his right, sold a dummy to the opposing half-back, and was off down the wing, weaving and dribbling past a succession of frustrated opponents, till, with a final superb body swerve, he crossed the ball square to the other pavement. Wattie gathered it in his stride, and first-timed it neatly between lamp-post and wall.

"Goal!"

They had to stifle the exultant shout. It was really too early in the morning.

"Good cross," Wattie conceded. "But did you see how I took it on the run? Masterly, masterly."

"Can I have your autograph, sir?" said Billy.

They issued from Black Street and crossed Parliamentary Road to Inglis's shop. Daddy Inglis had just unlocked the front door, and the other two delivery boys, Wee Eck McAusland and Aloysius Forde, known as Wishy, were grunting over the bulky parcels of newspapers which had been left in the doorway by the wholesaler's van. There was some horseplay as the four of them manhandled the stuff inside. Wattie laid Wee Eck across the counter and made a mock apology to Daddy Inglis.

"Sorry, sir! I thought he was one of the free gifts fell out of the *Red Star Weekly*."

Wee Eck, Alexander Wotherspoon McAusland, at fourteen was a three-foot-ten Gulliver in a world of five-foot Brobdingnagians. He was accustomed to this kind of joke, and had learned by bitter experience to take it in good part.

"If I could have a bit of help down off this sheer drop," he said timidly, "I could maybe get on with the work."

"Ah yes, the work!" Daddy adopted his pseudo-parental style. He was actually a bachelor, and childless. "Now, now, lads…" his hands going through the motions of patting heads, "…the workers of Glasgow are waking. The Townhead is hungry for its news."

The papers unpacked, each delivery boy began to make up his own round. By now, Billy was familiar enough with his to have little need for the shiny black notebook which contained names, addresses, and the papers on order; but he kept it open in front of him anyway. There were always the weekly magazines to be added to the daily round, and these he wasn't yet sure of. It was no great strain though, and he always enjoyed this part of the routine.

16

The shop fascinated him. It was Aladdin's cave, a shadowy vault filled with strange treasures, a bazaar of smells. One wall was entirely made of penny bundles of firewood. It was guarded by the two barrels of soft soap – one of green, one of black – with their hygienic aura of healthy, disinfected cleanliness, and flanked by the great, smelly drum of paraffin. The counter was mostly taken up by newspapers and periodicals, but there was space for the rope-like coil of Thick Black, for the wooden-handled guillotine that sliced it up, half-ounce by half-ounce, and for the little balances with the set of highly polished, circular, brass weights which measured it out. The smell of Thick Black, of Walnut Plug, of Brown Twist, or the threepenny-worths of snuff – light brown, brown, and black – weighed out in home-made paper pokes, was an alchemist's brew, a broth of tantalising complexity.

To Billy, all this symbolised the sight, sound and smell of the adult world he had so recently entered. It was there as a sort of dream background which he savoured with the tip of his mind as he collected papers and paired them with names.

Lawson, 250 Taylor Street, *Daily Record*...

A name, an address, a paper, and also a journey through a narrow, brown-painted close lit greenly by a flickering gas-lamp, up a dark stairway spiralling for three stories, with six doors to each shadowy landing, and some with letter boxes, and some without. He still felt a faint aftertaste of worry left over from his initial difficulty with nameplates in the poor light.

Nameplates! Nameplates and the poetry of names. Mostly they were an admixture of Scots and Irish: McDonald, O'Neill, McGregor, O'Mara, Docherty, Bruce, Campbell, Nolan, Ogilvie, but there was the occasional Smith, and one or two foreigners like Snodgrass and Shufflebotham.

He reached McManus, 112 Parson Street, *Bulletin*, and tried to regard it as nonchalantly as he had the rest, but he had been conscious of its approach before he came to it, and the name triggered a flash of red cardigan behind his eyes, and gave him a quick, teasing glimpse of the mobile curve of her cheek as she smiled her thanks. He stumbled on, the rhythm broken, the pattern agley...

Brennan, 110 Parson Street, *Daily Sketch*...

Of the four of them, only Eck, his left arm too short to encompass the thick bundle of papers, used a bag for his deliveries. Billy and Wattie paused for a moment and watched him as he crossed Parliamentary Road almost at a run beside the rock-stocky Irish figure of Wishy Forde. He ran as though he were a yacht with feet, heeling to starboard against the weight of the green canvas satchel.

"How the hell does he climb stairs," asked Wattie, "without finishing up inside the bag?"

"Probably leaves it in the close," said Billy. "He might be wee, but he's not an idiot, and he works as big a round as the rest of us."

They separated, each with his armful of enlightenment for those decaying stone bastions of working-class respectability, the tenements of Townhead.

Billy turned into Taylor Street and began his zig-zag, close-by-close progression towards the brow of the hill and the left wheel into Parson Street. Automatically, his mind adopted the posture which had become a familiar part of the routine. The numbers on the closes suggested the names of the customers, the papers they took, how many stairs up they lived. He counted steps with the uncommitted, rhythmic part of his brain, turned right or left into cavernous lobbies, and inserted folded newspapers into slits of letter boxes. Often he had to push hard against the spring-loaded brass flaps and the dragging weight of clothing hung behind the doors, and sometimes, when there was no letterbox, he knocked the door and delivered his charge directly to a reluctant, early-morning face.

"Paper! Thank you!"

It was a ritual phrase, almost a song, as indeed the counting of stairs was a song, and the whistling under his breath was a song. It passed the time, it helped him on his round, it left some other part of his mind free to think, or feel, or whatever it was that happened when he reacted so disturbingly to the mystery of the dark morning.

He had never thought about her – not thought – not the kind of thing you did when you read a book from left to right, word by word, and worried the meaning out of it. He had strange, inexplicable visions of the brightness and colour of her against the light of the gas, and her shape framed in the doorway. He had dreamed of her as something held close to him and longed for with a heart-hammering, blood-pounding intensity.

But, till now, he had not thought – not thought.

She was old – not old like his mother, who was over thirty – but old, in her twenties maybe. She was... She was... the woman of the house...

248, Balfour, *Daily Record*, two up, right...

243, Logan, *Daily Express*, three up, left...

240, Munro, *Daily Mirror*, close, middle door...

And then it was Parson Street, and then it was number 112, and then it was McManus, one up, right, *Bulletin*. Very little light from the stairhead lamp reached round into the wooden lobby, but even so, it was obvious that the door was the same drab, chewed-up door as all the rest. It, of course, had no letterbox. He knocked.

There were some scuffling sounds. The door opened and gaslight streamed out into the landing. The man who stood there was short, broad, and in his semmit. Black hair matted the chest, shoulders, and thick forearms.

"Paper! Thank you!" Billy sang, and the hand which took it from him had short, powerful, spatulate fingers.

The door closed and Billy turned towards the stair. He still had more than half his round to do. Through the staircase window he noticed that the patch of sky above the back court was turning grey. For a moment he seemed to get a half-glimpse of a powerful hand with thick, fumbling fingers, then it was gone. He took the remaining stairs three at a time and went out of the close whistling under his breath.

# Anything in Trousers

Wattie spent a whole week in the tailoring trade. It was never quite clear whether, when he left it, he was lured by the promise of a job in engineering or driven away by the laughter and the knowing looks of the two benches of trouser machinists vociferously led by Big Maud Tighe. One of life's natural enthusiasts, he had certainly liked the idea of going to work in the clothing factory, and his last day at Inglis's shop had been spent in a stew of impatience.

"I'll be looking for a suit of clothes wholesale when you become a journeyman," remarked Daddy Inglis as he paid Wattie the last wage he was to earn as a newspaper boy.

Wattie, who thought a journeyman must be some kind of travelling salesman and was therefore puzzled by the allusion, nevertheless assumed the man-to-man air he regarded as appropriate to one about to enter the great world of commerce and manufacture.

"No doubt something can be arranged, Mr. Inglis," he said. "I'm thinking of taking up the pipe, and I'd expect my tobacconist to be decently dressed."

The pseudo-parental pat on the head that Daddy Inglis was wont to bestow threatened to become a clout on the ear, but Wattie was off. He joined Billy on the pavement outside and they crossed towards Black Street.

"An old Jessie!" Wattie said. "We should have called him Granny Inglis."

"Ach! He's not a bad old stick," Billy protested; but Wattie had ceased to listen. Again he bubbled over in anticipation of the new job.

"I'm fairly looking forward to Monday," he enthused. "Bags of machinery, and you should see the dames – thousands of them."

As a description of the factory floor of S. Rose & Co., Clothing Manufacturer, Dobbie's Loan, this was neither complete nor accurate. It would have taken a lot more than the brief glimpse

Wattie had been given, during his interview with Mr. Levine, to enable him to paint a more detailed picture. In fact, he wheeled many a skepful of pieces out of the cutting room and distributed them among the long benches of machinists before the first impression of a vast, organic body of noise resolved itself into separate cells of sound, and the pervasive odour of the place became recognisable as the compound of many individual smells.

Noise and smell; these were the first and most apparent characteristics of the factory. It produced clothing – jackets, waistcoats, trousers – and it did so with a screaming roar that spun your head, and in a stench that nauseated you, unless you were an old hand and had allowed two of your senses to be blunted beyond awareness; or unless you were a very new hand like Wattie who, from sheer enthusiasm, was able to listen through the noise and sniff beyond the smell.

The basic underlying rumble, he discovered, was generated by the motor-driven shafts which ran between the pairs of benches and transferred motion by belt to machine. These gave off the smell of power: cold steel, warm bearings, hot oil, balata, vulcanite. The whirring was a hundred seams run up on a hundred sewing machines, the snipping, a hundred threads cut by a hundred pairs of scissors. The vinegary smell was from the dressing used in pocket linings and the buckram that was sewn as stiffening into trouser flies, waistbands and jacket fronts. The clack-clack-clack was the sound of the buttonholer, and the sustained buzz was the bandknife cutting cloth, and when the cloth was Harris Tweed, the smell was peat. The steam irons and the Hoffman presses thumped and hissed and filled the air with the aroma of wet wool. And over all, the incessant waves of female conversation, and the vaguely acrid odour of sweating female bodies.

As much as anything else, Wattie enjoyed the singing. One of the older women, as she worked at her machine, would be humming away at 'The Rose of Tralee' or 'Love's Old Sweet Song' when, first her own bench, then the entire floor would take it up, and for a time the noise of the machinery would be drowned in sweetness and harmony. As he aimed his laden skep up the narrow passage that ran along the ends of the benches, and threw bundles of stock and specials on to the checker's tables, Wattie found himself breathing the sentimental old songs.

He knew them well, for his mother loved the Music Hall and was a good kitchen soprano to boot. He himself went a lot to the pictures, so he was also no stranger to the numbers the younger machinists sang. Under his breath he was Bing Crosby in 'The Blue of the Night' and could do a surreptitious Nelson Eddy to 'Rosemarie' and 'The Indian Love Call'.

The two end benches, the trouser machinists, were great for the singing, and in this, as in all else, it was Big Maud Tighe who took the lead. Big Maud had a glorious voice. A description of it was, more or less, a description of Maud herself: large, untutored, unrefined, but warm and with a laugh in it; a sort of gallus contralto. She could community-sing with the best of them; but when Chrissie McGarrity or Theresa MacIvor addressed her specifically – "Give us a song, Maud" – it was her extensive repertoire of bawdy ballads they were referring to, and it was with one of those that Maud would oblige.

> I am a Dundee weaver and I come frae Bonny Dundee.
> I met a Glesga fella and he came courtin me.
> He took me oot a-walkin doon by the Broomielaw
> And then the dirty wee rascal took ma thingummyjig awa

Her audience would take up the repeat of the last line, their scissors beating out the tempo on the tops of their machines.

> And then the dirty wee rascal took ma thingummyjig awa

It was usually at about this point in the proceedings that Mr. Levine appeared, particularly if the girls were engaged on 'specials' he wanted out in a hurry. He bounced up and down the lines of benches creating, more than ever, the impression that he was in a perpetual state of sweaty excitement.

"No singing," he squeaked. "No talk, work hard, no singing."

The import of Big Maud's reply was lost on him as he disappeared like a corpulent rabbit into his cubbyhole of an office.

"Away and dally up a lamp-post!" she cried.

A long life spent immured in clothing sweatshops had confirmed Mr. Levine in a profound ignorance of the human female in general and the female machinist in particular. All machinists, he was convinced, had two attributes in common: they were mad, and they were lazy. Some of them were also coarse, lascivious, criminal, weak-minded, malicious, man-mad or money-mad or both or some or all of these things. It was necessary, at any rate, for him to appear in the midst of them periodically and exhort them to greater efforts. He was wrong about this. These girls were on piece work and inspection was meticulous. To make a living they had to keep their heads down. Maud was probably one of the best trouser machinists in the factory. She regularly lifted thirty to thirty-five shillings a week, and at fourpence a pair for stock and about a shilling a pair for specials she was slinging no lead. Actual relaxation, in spite of the singing, was unknown until the power was switched off for the tea break.

It was Moosie Brown, a fifteen-year-old with three months more service than Wattie, who warned him about the tea break and the effects of relaxation on the two end benches, and of the dangers confronting uninitiated new boys caught in their vicinity with the power off. He had a fund of horrific tales, many of them no doubt apocryphal, of naked legs seen kicking frantically over the edges of empty skeps, of backsides with a lipstick-painted eye on each buttock, of trousers forcibly removed and returned later with the leg holes stitched across and a patch fitted over the fly buttonholes. Some of his descriptions were so lurid that Wattie was frankly sceptical.

"It take a right sissy to let a few dames work a flanker on him."

"Don't you believe it," advised the sagacious Moosie. "When there's about twelve of them holding you down, it wouldn't matter supposing they were midgets; and anyway, have you seen Big Maud? She's got muscles like Johnny Weismuller. She could eat you for tea break and spend the rest of the morning spitting the seeds out between her teeth."

"Like to see her try," said Wattie.

Brave words, and of course, apprehensive though he might be, they had to be reinforced by demonstrations of temerity. Besides, there was a certain fascination in flouting danger, and an excitement in the thought that, at any moment, real women might hurl themselves upon him and bear him to the ground with their real arms and their real legs and their real breasts. However, they were, after all, only dames, and in the duelling which ensued every time he delivered trouser stock to the checker's table, he held his own.

"Aw! It's my own wee darlin Wattie." This was Chrissie McGarrity. "How's about you an me gettin married?"

"I'm sorry, Madam," said Wattie solemnly, "I promised first refusal to Big Maud."

"I'll Big Maud ye," cried Big Maud. "Less of your cheek or I'll have your guts for garters."

"My favourite position," said Wattie, manoeuvring his empty skep for getaway. "Halfway up to heaven."

Big Maud laughed as heartily as everyone else on the bench at Wattie's Parthian shot, but there was an air of finality in the way she spoke when the laughter died away.

"Right, girls," she announced. "It's the bottle treatment for that one. Remember now, first tea break he's up this way."

And the very next day was Wattie's Waterloo. He made the tactical error of being caught with an armful of unmade trousers at the checker's table when the power went off for tea break. The factory suddenly became a squealing, female chaos full of bulging cotton overalls, smooth legs and spiky heels, broad hips, strong arms, coloured hair and all the world's weight of women pinning him like paralysis to the floor. He felt rough hands upon his trouser flies and the shock of his flesh being inserted into the cold, narrow neck of a glass bottle.

"It's not coming up." The distant voice was Chrissie McGarrity's.

"I'll fix that," said Big Maud. She stood over Wattie, one foot at each side of his head. "How's that for a view?" she bawled, and she sank slowly down on her knees until her great, fleshy thighs almost touched his face.

"It's rising, it's rising," cried Chrissy McGarrity; but at that moment the air was pierced by a terrible scream and Big Maud hurled herself away from Wattie's supine figure like a rock from a Roman Ballista.

"The wee bugger's bit me," she yelled.

The hands that held Wattie loosened in surprise. He shook them off, scrambled to his feet, tucked in semmit, shirt, bottle and all, and ran for it. A blur of laughing female faces lined his path, his every step was derisively echoed by a hundred pairs of scissors rapped on a hundred bench-tops. The factory acknowledged him.

"By Jesus, Maud!" said Chrissie McGarrity. "Tide marks is one thing, but what's Paddy McGuffie gonna say about teeth marks?"

"Paddy McGuffie can go and raffle his doughnut," said Big Maud, for the moment indifferent to the possible response of her intermittent steady. She massaged herself with more gentleness than modesty. "Imagine that Wattie. The wee Turk." Her eyes suddenly gleamed and her humour returned as she recalled the scene.

"Did you get a good look at him?" she demanded of the factory at large. "Give him a year or two and he'll break a few hearts." Her laugh rang out above the buzz of conversation. "I mean," she roared, "if the bottle doesn't break first."

# The Great Lover

Billy washed his hands and face, brushed his teeth, and examined his red eyelids in the spotted L.N.E.R. mirror. He felt only slightly better, for there was still the sour morning-after taste of Yorkshire Breweries Draught at the back of his throat, and the stiffness of corridor trains in his bones. Even at five in the morning Queen Street Station held the memory of too many goodbyes. It was not there to be enjoyed; it was the fringe of home, but not home, and while the previous night still hung about him, it was not even familiar.

In a sense he was nearer York than Glasgow. There was only the shrieking vacuum of the night train north between the two, and since he had not yet come to the one, it followed he had not quite left the other. The spotted mirror could just as easily have been the one he silently spoke into last night in the Coach and Horses, or was it the Dick Turpin Inn, or the Mucky Duck?

"Flight-bloody-Sergeant Billy boy, respected NCO in effing charge of Squadron Signals, with the war fizzling out, and the drains of Europe stapped with dead Germans…"

In best-blue instead of the customary battledress his reflection struck him as more theoretical than real, though his arm was the same glory of lightning flashes, gleaming brass crown, and triple chevrons.

To right and left of him Canadian aircrew stooged along at twenty thousand feet shooting lines to the hard-faced whores of York, to the lonely young matrons with husbands in the Middle East, to the beer-drinking WAAFs who'd heard it all before, and, in some sad cases, to each other. His own small swaying circle, cohering through friendship, their common purpose, and a single order at the bar, nevertheless tended to diffusion at the edges. Ronnie Redman, after his third beer, had taken to reciting Rupert Brooke in short ecstatic bursts like Rühr flak; Jack Mark, navigator and hellion from Bundaberg, Queensland, risked an inter-allied punch-up by telling a lascivious story to a couple of civvy bints giggling over Canadian-bought gin; Pat Preston stood four-square behind his pint jug and remained quietly and philosophically himself.

I have been so great a lover,

declaimed Ronnie, a little froth glistening on his upper lip,

> filled my days
> so proudly with the splendour of Love's praise,
> The pain, the calm, and the astonishment...

"We'll have to leave soon," said Pat, "just in case your train's on time. Let's have a last pint."

Billy handed over his glass abstractedly. He was interested in the Rupert Brooke but at the same time was straining to hear Jack's payoff line.

"Right, said the Colonel," the story ended, "I'll have the one with the flaming great tits."

Jack accepted the laughter as his modest due, handed over his empty glass, and turned a shrewd Australian ear to Ronnie's performance.

> ...And all dear names men use to cheat despair,
> For the perplexed and viewless streams that bear
> Our hearts at random down the dark of life...

And when at last they bore themselves more or less at random down the darkened streets of York towards the station, Jack twitted Ronnie about literary diarrhoea, and Ronnie remembered another four lines he had previously missed:

> ...Shall I not crown them with immortal praise
> Whom I have loved, who have given me, dared with me
> High secrets, and in the darkness knelt to see
> The inenarrable godhead of delight?

But it was Pat who squeezed Billy's shoulder almost confidentially and said: "You've been too long without leave, Bill. A couple of weeks with the wife and family and you'll sort yourself out. You'll see!"

And the train, though late, was inexorable.

There comes a time when you run out of escape routes, when the roads away from pain have all been blocked, when the last Halifax is down and the last Wireless Operator is debriefed. There comes a time when the Ronnies and the Pats and the Jacks recede to nothing on the long York platform and you upend your suitcase in what Ronnie would call 'the squaddie-clotted corridor' and settle into your greatcoat collar for the long night journey to the north, with only your weariness to sustain you, and only the beer fumes hanging between you and the sight of your own ignominy. There comes a time, as now, in this limbo between last night and today, when your mouth is full of the taste of toothpaste and you are trapped in the lonely menace of the hissing urinals.

Billy fastened his tunic and his suitcase and passed through the station into the dark wetness of Dundas Street. This was Glasgow in the blackout. The drizzle was on his left cheek as he turned north and headed up the hill across Cathedral Street to Parliamentary Road. As he turned east he decided to walk home. There was probably no option anyway. He couldn't remember from previous leaves whether the trams ran as early as they had done before the war. But his greatcoat seemed proof enough against the light drizzle, the walk would help clear the remaining fuzziness from his head, and there was the whole length of Parliamentary Road promising the renewal of early-morning acquaintance. Besides, it was a bit too early to be waking Jess and the boy...

Ahead ran the broad stream which had nourished his childhood, dark now, except where the hooded wartime lamps pocked the wet flags with yellow discs of light, and disguised by the anti-blast baffle walls at every close-mouth. What he actually saw was the memory of it, and what he heard in his mind were the brave ringing names of its tributaries. On the right going up: North Hanover Street, North Frederick Street, McAslin Street, St. James' Road and Murray Street, Taylor and St. Mungo, Glebe and Martyr; and on the left, Dobbie's Loan and North Wallace Street, Drummond, Lister, Ward, Black, Glebe and Hartfield.

...And all dear names men use to cheat despair...

He felt a faint twinge as though blood were beginning to circulate again in his numbed emotions. It was painful. He glanced, as he passed, up the cobbled shoulder of Hanover Street and realised with some slight shock how extremely familiar it was; not familiar like the view of a well-known landscape or a nod from a passing acquaintance; but familiar like the feel of an old suit or a worn pair of shoes, or like passing your tongue over the back of your teeth. The dirt between the cobbles was the same dirt that had stuck under his fingernails and become ingrained in the skin of his hands. The rain that ran down the sivers had mingled with his tears as a child. Perhaps more recent tears were the more bitter for having been washed by an alien rain. He shook off the fancy. He was related to this place. What he had been here had nothing to do with the war, nothing to do with the Air Force, nothing to do with the silent scream that came in the long emptinesses of the bomber's night after Marie had gone for good...

He knew Marie had gone for good – he carried the burden of her absence, and had suffered shock by the manner of her going – yet for long he was unable to accept the finality of it. The news of her marriage to Anderson, the Canadian pilot, had not ended it in his mind. It was another temporary fact, like the war itself, to be cold-stored away from the danger of significance. Her discharge from the WAAF had not ended it in his mind, nor her visit back to camp to say a last goodbye to her friends before she sailed for Canada. Nor had her last goodbye to him ended it in his mind.

She was waiting for him when he returned after takeoff. His minute office in the Squadron Signals Section contained a desk, a chair, an enormous blackboard showing the aircraft state, and a narrow bed erected for use during night operations. Here he was able to sleep with his head against the crackling RT, alert for the call from the first pilot back into the circuit. She was sitting on the bed, but stood up when he entered. It was the first time he had seen her dressed as a civilian, deliberately feminine, alluring, and the effect upon him was so poignant that for a while he was unable to speak. It was she who tremulously broke the silence.

"Bill!" She said.

"You're married," he stated with flat stupidity.

"So are you!" she flashed back at him, and in a moment they were together, their bodies straining, a feverish reaction against their hopelessness. He felt tears wet on his cheeks, but whether they were hers or his own he did not know, and for the time being he did not care. There was joy, and there was misery, and the two could fuse together into...

...The inenarrable godhead of delight...

29

St. James' Road! Billy looked along it, but it was still too dark to see more than a vague wet pool of shadow where stood the blackened red-sandstone bulk of Provanside Higher Grade School. It was here that he had been given two and a half years of secondary education. He had since forgotten all the French they had taught him; the maths he had done all over again during his apprenticeship; the English! Well, he remembered Miss Fraser, second-year English teacher who used to sit on a high stool in such a position that boys in the front rows could see her stocking tops. There was, he recalled, a great deal of jockeying for places before a period of English, and, during class, an inordinate amount of pencil-dropping. Yet she had succeeded in stirring his interest in EngLit, EngComp and prosody. They had never, as far as he could remember, done Rupert Brooke. He smiled, thinking of Ronnie Redman. Ronnie would have laid Miss Fraser on a soft bed and gently seduced her to the accompaniment of a quiet verse...

> Love is a flame:– we have beaconed the world's night.
> A city:– and we have built it, these and I...

It ended in his mind, he thought, when he received the letter from Canada:

"...It is over... Try not to think too harshly... I have told Colin about us and he has forgiven me..."

He read it through several times and finally allowed it to slip from his fingers into the coke stove. He took her photograph from his wallet and burned that too. There was now no vestige of tangible evidence that she had ever been. Tongues of flame were a purgative, then there was beer, then work, then remorse, then nostalgia, then a touch of Ronnie Redman and a flicker of Rupert Brooke. He was sorry for himself, sorry for Marie and for Colin Anderson and for Jess and the boy. A great wave of sorrow washed over him, sorrow for everybody in this filthy, stinking, futile, warring world, sorrow for men and women, sorrow for children, sorrow for those who were being bombed and those who were bombing, sorrow for all of God's creation, and sorrow for God who had to sit back and watch it dying of gangrene. He was sorry – and he came home.

Billy crossed the road and turned north into Glebe Street. His close was the last but one before you reached the canal. He climbed the three flights of stairs and put his key to the lock of the middle door. A short lobby led to the single apartment where he and Jess had shared the few intermittent periods of their married life, and where she had conceived and then borne the boy. He stood in the semi-darkness and let the sight and the sound and the smell of it gather round him. Home! He turned at a slight noise from the recessed bed.

"It's all right, Jess," he said. "It's me – Billy. I'm back."

# The Last Act

I am her private diary. I register her inner thoughts and her out-ward actions. I am the peg on which she hangs her personality, the pin which fixes her sense of existence. Before me she has no modesty, no shame, no inhibition. I am not any longer a man, I am an ear. To Delia, I am unreal, as unreal as Delia is to me.

I lie on this cot, in this boxroom, I look at the irrelevant cracks that vein the grey plaster of the ceiling, and I listen.

Delia comes up for the third time with the third customer. There is the third whispered conference on the landing, and the third scrape of the key in the lock. Within minutes, in the next room, the banal scene will be enacted for the third time tonight, and two ghosts, in the grip of a pitiful illusion, empty of significance, will dance their little death to the furtive creak of a bedspring.

I lie on this cot, and I look at the ceiling, and again I feel the approach of the creeping, spiritual paralysis. My thoughts flutter and die, flutter and die with the mind's momentum, inertia without mass, force without substance. In the first of my visions I saw the world's doom, in the last I see my own. I am doomed because I saw too much, too deeply. In a lunatic world only the sane are mad.

That bright morning of the first vision remains in the mind like a bruise. The early rush-hour crowd spewed from the subway and sprayed in every direction across St. Enoch Square, east and west along Argyle Street, north up Buchanan, and south to the river. Traffic thickened at the intersection, people knotted at the corners and trailed in attenuated strings along the pavements. I crossed the junction against the lights, and entered Buchanan Street. It stretched ahead of me, narrowing in accordance with the law of optics, like the sides of a long, tilted isosceles triangle. On paper it could be represented by two upright lines converg-ing. Perspective, the illusion of the third dimension, an artist's device to deceive the eye, a convention of representational art, a metaphor for the appearances of nature as seen by the lying eye.

What if the artist's eye should be deceiving the artist? What if it should force a fraudulent law of optics on his unsuspecting consciousness? What if the world is a flat screen, and all the perspectives merely lines converging into nothingness?

Of course I could walk up Buchanan Street and know I had passed through space, because time went by, and the vanishing point remained as far away as ever. But do I feel myself in space? If, by moving, I was constantly changing my viewpoint of the flat screen, would this not give the impression of depth, just as the artist can with his cones and triangles on a flat canvas?

Suddenly, out of the throb of the city, a single car horn sounded a long, isolated blare like a signal, and I found myself outside myself looking, in the brightness of the morning light, at the world as it is, flat and two-dimensional. I saw the people as ghost images shrinking as they moved upscreen, growing as they moved down, disappearing as they moved out of frame. I saw into their minds and hearts and knew the meaning of their flurry and hurry and bustle. I understood their rush to keep up with their sense of purpose, why they hung on desperately to their identities, built, brick by brick, the structure of their personalities, because I saw the unthinkable alternative. They sought anchors to reality where there was no reality. They were unreal, the world was unreal. It was one vast, flat, purposeless, meaningless illusion.

A flash of sunlight on a plate glass window across the pavement caught my eye. I turned and looked at my own reflection. It was flat and transparent.

I lie on this cot and watch myself wither away, and I listen. The professional sounds from next door have passed their climax, and are followed by silence.

"When a man's spent, you don't talk. He wants to be quietly ashamed for a bit." Delia has studied her customers. She is efficient. She is also soft, with a quick sympathy.

"Has the old bitch thrown you out?" She had on her vivid, working face when we collided on the stairs. "You're welcome to the boxroom until you can get fixed up."

I found myself in the boxroom with a request to stay out of sight if Delia should return with a gentleman friend, and instructions on where to find the tea things in the scullery.

"Is that all your luggage? I thought you painted or something."

"Not now."

"What do you do?"

"Nothing."

"Oh! Well, cheerio!"

And she was gone about her business. Delia's was a night-time business. She worked hard at being desirable, and it was a point of honour with her, as well as a matter of commercial interest, that she gave value for money. During daylight hours she uncoiled. She slept late, cleaned house and washed clothes, bought and cooked food, and talked. She talked a great deal. Talking was necessary to her. At first it was questions.

"Didn't you have some arty job up Buchanan Street?"

"Yes, advertising."

"What did you do?"

"Posters."

Why did I leave? Wasn't the money good? Didn't I get on with the boss? What kind of pictures did I paint in the room upstairs? Did I use nude models? Why did the landlady throw me out? The questions died for lack of satisfactory answers, and Delia came to accept me for whatever it was she though I appeared to be. There were no explanations that I could give her that would have enabled her to tag me. And things had to be tagged. Everything needs a label to invest it with an appearance of reality. It isn't enough for a man to be a man, a sentient being, to exist. He must be a Communist, or a Christian, or a plumber, or a Tom, or a Dick, he must be a collection of beliefs, or a set of activities, or a word on a document. He must have a label, for without a label he is nothing.

Delia had labels for everything. She was a *Courtesan*, or what ever the equivalent word was in her vocabulary. She was also *Delia*, and too proud of the name not to have invented it herself. She knew about *Life*, *Life* being the collection of labels her experience made it possible for her to recognise. I suppose I became *Lodger*, or *Artist*, but whatever it was, she resolved it without help from me, for there were no explanations I could give her.

The posters, always slightly ridiculous, became absolutely farcical. Great, flat slabs of colour lay dead on the paper and mocked my life with their lifelessness. I sat for long periods staring at the shapes in desperation, unable to tinker with them any more. It wasn't just that they were dead. They had never lived. They were anti-life, and they infected me with an insidious, despairing paralysis. I tore myself free, and rushed out into that other fantasy world of Buchanan Street.

My painting, my "creative work", I once called it, decayed. For a while I tried to recreate objects as they really are, but the canvasses became a confused mass of perspectiveless planes and meaningless collages. I pruned and erased, incised, selected and rejected, until the whole philosophy of my creative work could have been represented by an idiot dot randomly splotched in the middle of a blank canvas.

I stopped painting. I stopped everything. I lay down and felt as though I weren't there. The long days passed and nothing happened. Sometimes I would go out into the streets and walk. I looked at things: a red skirt billowing in the wind, the veined hand of an old woman poised and motionless as she reached for the handrail of a bus. Movements were a series of still pictures flicked across the screen. Then someone would stare at me and I would flee. When they stare it makes me a labelled object. It draws the existence out of me. I fled to my room, until the day came when I was evicted, and Delia, the vivid, working Delia, gave me the boxroom, and the cot, and the scullery where the tea things were.

I lie on the cot in the boxroom, I look at the irrelevant cracks that vein the grey plaster of the ceiling, and I listen.

The final customer has felt his little shame and departed. The sound of running water indicates that Delia is washing. She will don the armoury of hair curlers that is so essential to the maintenance of her personality, and she will go to bed.

And I know what I must do.

The knowledge of the unreality of things has become the knowledge of my own unreality. I face it at last. I have not found my own existence, because I have not chosen to exist. I have not the will to exist. I must do something real. I must find the reality of myself by destroying the unreal. I must, by some last act, give myself dimension.

And I know what I must do.

I have rehearsed it. The razor is in my pocket. I shall put out the light and wait. In an hour she will be asleep. I will walk quietly into her room. She will be visible in the light from the street lamp outside. Her face will be pale against the pillow, her hair in strange, coiled shapes under the accoutrements. She will be lying on her back, her personality drained away by sleep, an imaginary being without a label. I will draw the razor across her neck, and the illusion will be gone.

But the act... Won't the act be real?

# A Therapy of Camels

I confess to some irritation when I recognised Archie McIlraith standing at the camel enclosure. Strangers milling around while I commune give me no concern, but a kent face is inhibiting. My purpose, after all, is a sort of self-flagellation, and no one likes to have his bottom smacked in front of friends.

I visit camels occasionally to treat my misanthropy. They are so supercilious, so contemptuous of everything human that, within half an hour, my native humility snaps back into place and I return to the cold-war comfort of my familiar neuroses. Camels bring perspective, and speculations on the correct collective noun for their groupings or words to describe the noise they make are fascinating and therapeutic.

This time, however, it looked as though my prophylaxis was in danger. I contemplated slipping away before Archie saw me, but my need was like the mainliner's need for a fix. Resignedly I approached and handed him the fancy-meeting-you-after-all-this-time routine, and was rewarded by the impression that he was not too pleased to see me. It was mutual.

Nothing personal of course. We accepted the inevitable, leaned our elbows on the rail, and surrendered to camels and conversation.

"Do they help," I asked, egotistically assuming that his reasons for being here must be similar to my own.

"Help?"

"The camels: the large, hornless, ruminant, long-necked, cushion-footed quadrupeds from the Concise Oxford."

"What d'ye mean, help?"

"I mean, do they ease the situation? Do they drain away the bile?"

"What bile?"

I tried again. "Have you noticed the sexual symbolism? The Arabian is purely phallic, the Bactrian is mammary. Or are you more interested in the religious significance?"

"Religious significance?"

I had left him behind somewhere. His obtuseness and his vacuous repetitions of my key phrases were becoming a bore. I gave him the works, Henke's poem and all:

> ...those fringèd humps,
> Like twin Franciscans
> Reluctant to be tonsurèd,
> And kept unkempt
> For penance...

"You're mad," he said. "And besides, I didn't come here to see camels. I came to meet somebody."

Silence...

Mine was the vacuum that exists between my manic phase and my depressive. His was morose.

"Heard you were married," I offered finally.

This innocuous observation seemed to startle him. I had touched an exposed nerve.

"Oh aye! Nearly two years now. Is it really that long since we last met?"

"I suppose so. How is married life?"

He ignored my question and instead asked one of his own: "Did you ever get married, Hamish?"

I had one of my spasms. It happens that I am subject to periodic surges of psychic cognition, spontaneous clairvoyant insights which I do nothing to evoke and over which I have little control. This one was typical, a subliminal awareness neither linear nor sequential, and therefore not to be scanned as words are scanned, a sort of instant programming, which, if it could have issued from my mind as a punched card and been fed to a computer, might have translated thus:

You, Archie McIlraith, having suddenly realised that I belong to your pre-marital past, see in me, a friend who is ignorant of (and therefore unprejudiced about) your recent history, a possible candidate for the confessional. Already your moroseness is evaporating as you concentrate on forming the words you are about to pour into my sympathetic ear. Your question to me was put, not out of interest in my situation, but as an introduction to your own agony, whatever that may be. Your next words will lead us straight to the problem.

"You've never met Lottie, have you?" he said.

"Your wife?"

"Yes. Lovely girl. Young, perhaps, but..."

And he told his story...

It was not precisely a whirlwind courtship – you don't associate Archie with whirlwinds – but, though young, Lottie was apparently decisive, and they were on honeymoon long before Archie would have, in the normal course of events, reached the stage of cautioning himself into a judicious postponement. Not that he had any regrets. Far from it. The honeymoon was a great success. Lottie was delightful. Effervescing with a youthful vitality, she was, nevertheless, intelligent and loving, eager to please, yet not over-submissive, mindful of his desires, his needs, his feelings, his opinions, yet not subservient to them. Delightful!

If he had any misgivings, it was because their future was not quite so cut-and-dried as his Scots canniness would have demanded. In the absence of a home of their own they were to begin their married life living with Millie.

Millie and Lottie were much closer, Archie thought, than was usual with mother and daughter. It was not the closeness of sisters either. "Almost uncanny," was the phrase he used. Admittedly they had, in a sense, grown up together, for Millie had been very young when her husband died just before Lottie was born. He felt, however, that this did not quite explain the rapport that existed between them. There was apparently no possessiveness in it, for Millie had accepted her daughter's marriage with equanimity. Certainly she had inspected him – a searching examination he remembered – but that was no more than a mother's prerogative.

Yes, he liked Millie and he got on well with her. But she was now, after all, his mother-in-law, and living in the same house might precipitate the banal situation which is so corny on the stage, but so often and so fearfully true to life. It wasn't really a worry, no more than a wisp of cloud on tomorrow's eastern horizon, and in the euphoria generated by the honeymoon and by Lottie, even that yielded to the warmth of the sun.

At this point in the narrative, Archie paused and gazed between the swaying humps of the nearest Bactrian to some memory situated in the middle-distance. He was honeymooning again and Lord knows to what erotic lengths he might have gone had I been content to leave him to his fantasy. "But your misgivings were justified," I prompted.

"Oh no!" He snapped back to the present. "The very opposite. It worked out extremely well."

After the honeymoon, Lottie went on with her course at the Art School. She was only a year away from her diploma, and it would have been a pity not to take it. It was pleasant, though, to come home in the evening to a bright fire and a beautifully-cooked meal, and Archie was not ungrateful for Millie's domestic talents. Nor indeed was he blind to her tact, her good nature, her generosity.

Her generosity…

"I have waited these months," she said, "because I wasn't sure that you would like it here. I thought maybe you would have ideas about a house of your own, and I didn't want to interfere."

"I love it here," Archie said.

"I would like to sign the house over to you."

"What?"

"Well, you are the man of the family now, Archie, and a man should be master of his own household."

Just then Lottie came in from the kitchen and he caught the quick gleam which passed from her eye to Millie's. It was their telepathy again. He was sure Lottie knew about the house without having to be told, and without having heard a word of the discussion.

This empathy between the two women was of great interest to Archie. He could cite dozens of little experiences which illustrated the unusual extent to which they invisibly communicated. They would each begin to hum the same tune at the same time, one would casually rise to fulfil some unspoken wish of the other, Millie would have the door open before Lottie had rung the doorbell. That kind of thing, only extended well beyond the limits set by acute hearing, intelligent anticipation, or coincidence. Archie remembered one occasion when Lottie's hand accidentally brushed against his own and he gave it an affectionate squeeze, only to surprise the quick, flushed smile of response on Millie's face.

"We were always close," Lottie explained, which was not really an explanation, and in time he became used to the phenomenon. In fact, to a strictly limited extent, he was able to share in it. Apparently telepathy, in common with other mental aberrations, can be infectious. This was only one aspect of a situation which, to Archie, appeared idyllic.

"Being a Libran," he said.

"Being a what?"

"A Libran. You know, Libra, the scales, lover of peace, postponer of decisions, and so on. I was perfectly happy."

It wasn't that he was overruled or dominated. On the contrary, he was deferred to, his opinion was sought, his position as head of the household was never in dispute. Fortunately, perhaps naturally, his decisions, his opinions, usually coincided with the general consensus. He quiesced. He is an acquiescent man, by his own account, a Libran. He was fulfilled. Life was good. In fact, it couldn't have been better. Or so he thought until a certain fateful Thursday morning.

He remembered it was a Thursday because that is the day he stays at home and clears up the week's paperwork. On this occasion he was enjoying a long lie in bed. Lottie had already gone for her bus, and he was indulging in one of those rambling, near-the-surface dreams which are the more luxurious because you know they won't be terminated by an alarm bell. There was a light knock on the bedroom door and Millie came in carrying a tray. He was vaguely aware of the tray being placed on the bedside table, the touch of her hand on his shoulder, and the sound of her voice.

"Tea, Archie."

He opened his eyes to her firm, gentle face with its aureole of brown hair and morning sunshine, and he knew, suddenly and devastatingly, that Millie had become engulfed in the overflow of his love for Lottie. He kissed her, and she responded, and it seemed natural that she should be beside him in the bed and they should be making love.

The week's paperwork had to wait until the afternoon on that Thursday, and indeed, on many Thursdays to come.

I stopped Archie right there. "What about Lottie?" I wanted to know.

"She knew," he said. "She didn't ask, and she wasn't told, but she knew, and she approved."

"You can't mean it."

He ignored my incredulity. "When she came home that evening she took one look at Millie, and she knew. It was as if they had shouted the news across the room to one another. She kissed me, then she kissed Millie, then she put her arms around the both of us, and we stood laughing in the centre of the room, a joyous trinity."

Archie's poetic imagery stuck in my gullet.

"They were always close," I contributed.

His glance was disdainful. "I know what your thinking..." I hoped not. "...but you're wrong. It was nothing like that. It was never spoken about. There was none of this three-in-a-bed stuff."

His eyes once more displayed a tendency to shoot off beyond the camel humps to some visionary limbo. When he spoke again it was as much to the hairy, Bactrian Alps as to me.

"All that love," he mused, "all that sweetness, all that perfection. More than I deserve. More than any man deserves. More than I can stand."

I had my mouth open ready to cut in as soon as he stopped slobbering, for the appropriate Freudian jargon had just occurred to me, when my eye was caught by a wondrous piece of yellow-coiffured miniskirt standing at the end of the camel enclosure waving furiously in the direction of Archie.

"Archie!" I exclaimed. "That's not..."

"No, no," he said quickly. "Just a friend." And with a muttered farewell he was off.

I watched them march away arm in arm into the distance. Just a friend! Who, I wondered, could be just a friend to anyone in that skirt, with that hair, with those legs...

I shrugged them goodbye and hitched myself back onto the enclosure rail. I think I hinted before that I am not really fond of camels. It's just that a half-hour in their company is salutary. And that noise they make, could it be, do you think, a derisive laugh?

# Dispossessed

The curt sentence uttered by the black-bearded Mill stopped Raymond where he stood. Jacqueline, Mill's darkly beautiful sister, whose wan face and haunted eyes had seemed to issue a mute invitation, stepped away from her brother's side and signalled Raymond to follow. He hesitated and glanced enquiringly in the direction of the black beard. Mill shrugged and spread his hands.

"It's your dream," he said.

Your dream!

The sudden excited urge was qualified in Raymond's mind by a faint disappointment. They were figments. Mill's brooding power was a fantasy in the unconscious, Jacqueline's attraction a sort of auto-eroticism. Already the vividness of their presence had diminished. They had slipped imperceptibly into the background, become shadowy, dreamlike.

Your dream!

> ...To dream, and realise one is dreaming fulfils the conditions for two-tier consciousness, the dichotomy most conducive to dissociation...

Raymond could have quoted verbatim the salient paragraph from Scheidegger.

> ...A small further effort of will, and projection is achieved...

He suppressed his excitement. A small further effort of will would demand calm and concentration. After his many failures this was too good an opportunity to spoil by over-eagerness. Carefully he examined his situation.

"I am here," he thought, "active and sentient, aware of my surroundings, and aware that they belong to a dream."

He was, therefore, asleep. Somewhere, just beyond the range of his present consciousness, he lay beside Beth's sleeping form in the bedroom of their semi-detached at No 28. Already he was outside. Projection was surely just a matter of realising he had projected. There remained one final step to take, one small further effort of will. Eyes closed, he strove to reduce the tempo of his thought, to channel his thinking, to specify his aims. Slowly, piece by piece in his mind, he assembled an image of the bedroom, its wallpaper, its curtains, carpet, wardrobe, dressing-table, bed. Each segment became an entity, each entity he scrutinised, lingered over, until it was invested with the glow of reality. He willed himself inside the room, to feel in his own breast its living pulse, as though its atmosphere surrounded him, as though he had only to open his eyes...

He opened his eyes. From a point high in the corner by the window he looked down at the bed. There he saw Beth, her face disembodied by the blankets, rendered pale, innocent, and vulnerable by sleep; and next to her, on the same pillow, he saw himself.

"What a shock," he told Beth next morning. "Funny! I've read so many descriptions, I'd have sworn I was prepared. And yet, when you stand outside and look at your own body lying there, it gives you the eeriest feeling."

"It would frighten the life out of me." Beth gave an involuntary shiver. "Raymond, I don't think you should dabble with this sort of thing."

"Nonsense! It's completely safe when you know what you're doing, and I've studied the subject. I'm not dabbling." Something in the set of her shoulders as she busied herself with the breakfast made him regret his momentary irritation. "Besides," he went on, "it may be no more than a queer twist to a dream."

"But I thought..."

"Yes I know. At the time it was real, all right. But in daylight... well, dreams are like that, aren't they?"

It was a concession to Beth's fears and Raymond knew it. He was as convinced as the daylight self can be of the reality of his nocturnal experience. Already he had half-decided the symbology he would employ to trigger off his next projection. Of course there was no harm in the corroboration of a simple independent test, a message left in a locked room, perhaps. Beth could help there. He would work on it. He would work on Beth. Given time, he knew, she would co-operate.

Given time...

Triumph warmed Raymond when he opened his eyes and

recognised the living room. His ability to see clearly every detail in the dark had by this, his fourth essay into the astral, ceased to astonish him. The thrill was one of achievement. Beth had locked this door and hidden the key from him before they went to bed. He had projected, willed himself into a sealed room, penetrated its walls as though they didn't exist. With practice, there was probably no place he couldn't visit. At present there remained only the message to find, Beth's message, which he had to memorise and take back to her in the morning. He found it within a few moments. On the mirror above the sideboard, drawn in soap, the traditional heart pierced by an arrow, and beneath it in large print,

## BETH LOVES RAYMOND

He smiled to himself. It was typical of Beth to appear light-hearted over something that worried her. This was her message right enough, affectionate, almost flippant, but he knew her too well not to detect the undertones.

"Beth loves Raymond," it really said, "and wishes he would stay beside her when asleep, instead of undertaking those lonely, and maybe even dangerous voyages into the unknown."

"Women", he said to the mirror, "have no scientific curiosity."

"Women", the mirror answered, "don't need it."

Raymond wheeled and presented an open mouth to the two figures standing by the closed door.

"You mustn't look so obviously disappointed, Raymond," the tall man said, white teeth flashing through the black beard. "This time it isn't a dream."

Raymond's look was not one of disappointment. It was a bewildered mixture of wonder and amazement, fear and disbelief. Mill and Jacqueline, brother and sister; twin figments, surely, of his imagination, creatures of his creating. Who were they? What were they? Real? Unreal? He ran out of question marks.

Jacqueline, whose large, sombre eyes, set wide in the strikingly pale face, issued that unmistakeable appeal, stepped away from her brother's side and signalled Raymond to follow. He hesitated and glanced enquiringly in the direction of the black beard. Mill shrugged and spread his hands.

"It's your life," he said.

Raymond followed Jacqueline, which is to say he did no more

than focus his attention on her, and something happened to him. He felt a sensation of movement, a shift, not through space exactly; a mental lurch. It was an intensified version of the projection experience, except that, whereas he determined the one, he was subservient to the other. At the end of it he found himself alone with Jacqueline in the centre of a large, dimly-lit, unfamiliar room.

"Where is this place?"

"Well, it's not actually a place."

He remembered with a start how stirred he was by the sound of this low, vibrant voice.

"Places are for bodies, and your body occupies its own place elsewhere. I, as you know, lost mine long ago."

Raymond did know. It was another fact, half-remembered from dreams, to be fitted into the complex that was this fascinating creature.

"But I see you."

"So you see me," she smiled. "Tell me then, what am I wearing?"

He was about to do so when he realised, with some shock, that she was naked. He gazed for a long moment as she stood there, effortlessly graceful, arms half-outstretched towards him. He measured the contrast of black hair cascading over white shoulders, followed the line of the pectorals to the small breasts, the gentle swelling curve of the abdomen, the dark smudge of the pubic triangle.

"You could touch me," she continued, "and I would feel solid, because you expect me to be solid. You could make love to me, and if you could recall forcibly enough the details of lovemaking, you could deceive yourself that it was real. But it would be mere fantasy. We are, at this moment, fantasising, or, as my brother would say, externalising our hallucinations.

Raymond had followed her speech somewhat inattentively, part of his mind still occupied with the promise apparent in her phantom nakedness. She gave him a long speculative look with those large, dark eyes which seemed to mock and to suffer at the same time.

"Let's go, my dear. Let's go and find some reality."

Again he had the feeling of motion, the fast pan of the mind's camera, the shift in the spectrum of the senses. Presently he heard the sound of distant music, a hum of voices, the flicker across the eyelids of shadowy figures moving. He paid attention.

It was a party, and it had reached that inconclusive, early-morning stage when a few couples shuffle in the centre of the room approximately in time to the record player, while the remainder of the company, distributed around the place mostly in pairs, drink the lees of the many bottles, talk desultorily, neck with no great conviction, or merely lounge. Raymond was troubled by a certain vagueness, a lack of clarity in the scene, as though he were viewing it through fine muslin. He was more vividly aware of Jacqueline at his elbow. He felt the quickening of her interest, the increase in her natural tension. He sensed, rather than saw, the shine in her eyes, the quiver of her moistened lip.

"They are real, Raymond," she breathed. "They have bodies."

One couple in particular seemed to hold her attention. Young, barely out of their teens, they stood clasped together, swaying to the music, though apparently anchored to their position in one corner of the room. The boy was in shirtsleeves, stockily built, his back broad and sweating, arms thick, hair violently red. The girl was fair, pretty, big-breasted, leggy in the short-skirted modern manner, consciously nubile. Their dance was a rhythmic embrace. They were oblivious of everything but the beat of the music and their own proximity.

"Those two," Jacqueline murmured almost to herself. "The dancing pigeons." She turned to Raymond. "Here is stimulation for your scientific curiosity."

He was suddenly intrigued by his awareness of Jacqueline's intentions, and the knowledge, spontaneously generated it seemed, of how these were to be achieved, and of his own part in them. No more than a moment's qualm as to the ethics involved in what he was about troubled the surface of his mind. There was the fascination of the experiment itself, the clutch and promise of excitement, and there was desire. The novelty of remaining undetected in a crowded room reminded him of his childhood fancy on reading *The Invisible Man*, and there was enough of the child left in him to relish the superiority thus bestowed. As he approached the boy he summoned his psychic resources for an extreme, concentrated effort. His aim was conjugation, something more than mere empathy, a sort of mental symbiosis. He had to insinuate himself into the other's mind, to think as he thought, feel as he felt, to attain complete rapport with him, to become him.

It was much easier than Raymond had imagined it would be. Certainly there were strange, even frightening side-effects to be overcome. An unaccountable dizziness plagued him for a bit. Then a grinding buzz of pain in his skull, as though he were being trepanned, caused him momentarily to lose his grasp of the situation. Finally, after the feeling that his tongue was swelling and choking him had been rigorously controlled, he achieved his object.

The music thundered around him as he swayed. Sweat poured down his face and neck, and his shirt clung to his back. His throat held the wersh aftertaste of beer. He was exhilarated by the drink and the incessant beat, and inflamed by the urgency of the soft body pressed against him. He caught her glance and held it.

"Love you, Mary," he said hoarsely.

For an instant her small, blue eyes became larger, darker, flashed a mocking glint. Her short, crisp, fair hair liquefied, flowed over her neck in a blue-black cascade, and became shoulder-length.

"Love you, Sandy," she lisped, and the impression of metamorphosis was gone.

He gazed into her eyes, willing a response from he as he steered across the room and out into the hall where an overflow meeting performed the same rites as the main body. Scant attention was paid to them as he eased her gently into one of the bedrooms and closed the door behind him. The sudden transition to complete darkness hid Mary from his sight, and it was Jacqueline who led him over to the bed and pulled him down on top of her. It was Jacqueline whose questing tongue darted between his teeth, who pulled away their clothing, who laid a knowing hand upon his straining flesh. It was Jacqueline against whom and within whom he thrust himself.

"Love you, Jacqueline."

"Love you, Mary."

"Sandy!"

"Raymond!"

Love you, love you, love you, the throb and heat and sweat of love, the tender brutality of love, the rising tempo, the jig, the gavotte, the pushing and the biting and the frenzy...

A million miles away, in the high Sierras, an eagle screamed.

48

Lightning flashed vividly, and the sudden timpani of thunder rolled and reverberated round his head. Raymond felt his skull cleft open and hot sand pour over his brain. He was falling down a great, timeless curve into darkness.

He was back in his bedroom, familiar but different, back at the point high in the corner by the window, the same point but more remote, back looking down at the bed. There was Beth, his own Beth, pale, sweet, vulnerable, and beside her on the pillow, himself. As the vision shimmered and slipped away, he saw his own face harden, the eyes open, the white teeth flash through the black beard.

"No!" he screamed. "No!... No!..."

# The Moment

It was useless, they had knocked off for the night. Jimmy's fists ached from pounding the insulated door and his throat was gritty. He smiled, a little ashamed, when he thought of how he had shouted. Panic! Desperation! Claustrophobia! He shrugged.

Behind the thick, clinical walls the motor vibrated, so many revolutions per second, the pump oscillated and maintained compression, so many pounds per square inch, enough to vaporise refrigerant. Inside, the temperature fell, so many degrees below zero. How many? Twenty? Forty? Sixty?

Jimmy felt for his cigarettes and paused with the packet half open. The place was bound to be airtight. He made a quick mental estimate of cubic capacity, length by breadth by height, and wondered how to translate the result into breathing time. Regretfully he returned the cigarettes to his pocket.

"The Philosopher", his fellow-electricians called him. "Here comes the bloody philosopher", big Ferguson would say. "Put away your pools guides, you ignorant shower, the thinker is among us." A great joker, big Ferguson. Jimmy saw the column that would keep them from the back page for one morning:

### ELECTRICIAN DIES IN BUTCHER'S FRIDGE

The Philosopher, they called him. This was a situation for philosophy. He looked at the neat rows of carcasses and saw them, for the first time, as dead animals. Dead that we might live, they were now merely his predecessors, comrades gone before and waiting his arrival. He saw himself on the hook at the end of the line, hung in a state of arrested putrefaction, ready for consumption. The air, the limited air, had a definite chill.

The glowing oval of armoured glass, he decided, was friendly, but it was ironic that he had conscientiously slipped in at the last minute to replace the faulty lamp. If he hadn't done so, if he hadn't left the door ajar instead of opening it wide, if those damned butchers had only looked inside before closing up and switching on, if only, if only. It was a profitless avenue of thought. At least he had light, and even a minute source of heat. Within that oval glass was the only warm place in the room. He could cup his hands round it, not yet, but it might come to that.

His watch said six o'clock, thirteen, maybe fourteen hours before the first butcher began his day's work. Fourteen hours! At a pinch the air might last. Certainly the cold would. The inexorable beat of the pump would be interrupted only when the temperature fell below the pre-set limit on the thermostat. All too efficiently the cold would be maintained.

Died of exposure had an adventurous ring, like A Night on the Bare Mountain. But enclosed in the tiled walls of this disinfected cell, in company with these depersonalised, disembowelled corpses, death did seem a bit sordid and ignominious.

Six o'clock! He saw Bess moving about her kitchen, fussing over the dinner. Already he was overdue. "Daddy's late. Eat your potatoes", she told the kids. She ate nothing herself and sat knitting after the children were in bed. She wasn't exactly worried. "Unexpected overtime," she thought, "extra work after the holidays." Every few minutes she looked out of the window and down the road. Whom would she phone about ten o'clock? The police, finally, and they would check at the depot, find it closed, and contact old Gallacher. Gallacher would dither about, irritate everybody, and get nowhere. Only Bess would feel any urgency, and there was little Bess could do.

Six o'clock! Eight hours, ten hours, fourteen hours. What did it matter? At a pinch the air would last, though it would be a sight less fresh by morning. It was the cold that would kill him. Jimmy felt in his overalls and took an inventory of his tools: penknife, pocket screwdriver, side-cutters, junior hacksaw. Toys! Certainly not designed for digging a way through an insulated cave. His only hope was to stop the motor. The vibration on the walls mocked the thought. He didn't even know where it was. It was near, of course, behind the wall or under the floor. He could hear it and feel it, but it might as well have been in China. He could take the lamp out and short across the holder. Then what? Blow the lighting fuse, put the place in darkness and listen to the bloody motor chugging away.

The cold began to bite. The moisture in his nostrils crystallised. Funny to feel cold like this in the middle of the best summer for years. He looked at the lamp glowing in the frosted glass and remembered the sun over the Western Isles. They had looked forward to it for so long: the holiday: the reunion with his brother, John, and the sun had shone every day for a fortnight. Suddenly he felt lonely. And with the feeling came a sense of recognition, a familiarity with the moment that took him back to that sun-bleached day on the west coast of Lewis when he and John had strolled together along the white sand and tried to bridge years of separation in the kind of talk that would have sent big Ferguson up the wall. It was the continuation of an old topic between them.

"I always feel", John said, "when I walk the machair, this sensation of paradox, of being solitary and involved at the same time. There's a sense of being alone, and a sense of never being alone."

Jimmy thought he recognised what John was describing and put his own gloss on it. "There's a moment of crisis," he ventured, "a manifold moment containing fear, exaltation, wonder. It's a peak of feeling, a culmination which happens very seldom and, I suppose, to very few. One way or another, those who experience it must have attained to a critical pitch of sensitivity."

"And you've felt it?"

"I think it has lurked round the corner once or twice, especially during the war."

And John gave him a copy of 'Summer Day On Lewis', a poem he had recently written.

> Seen from the machair's edge
> miles of white sand swathe north.
> The light is Greek (I'm told).
> The green Atlantic merely
> whispers of America.
>
> Two black dots in the distance
> move and grow, a couple
> strolling towards me along the sand.
>
> We are an infinity apart
> which takes eternity to cross.
>
> "Nice day", he says, and she, smiling,
> offers, "What a lovely beach."
>
> I leave my cosmic survey
> to hear myself reply:
> "A little crowded."

The cold was almost unbearable now. The room was filled with the steady beat of the motor. The enemy had a voice. Soon the nadir of temperature would be reached and the motor would cease to turn, would hold its malice in abeyance, be silent for a space, voiceless and deadly. The cold was pain. That was safe. He had read of exposure and knew that danger lay in the warmth that crept over you, in the pleasant drowsiness that lulled you to a long sleep. He must remain active, keep his mind clear. He must think.

Power dissipated is proportional to the square of the current. An induced current, by virtue of its electromagnetic effect, always tends to oppose the force which produced it. Parallel lines are equidistant from each other at all points along their length. Parallel lines, two lines, two pipes that ran the length of the wall opposite, two pieces of conduit, feeds that led through the wall to... what? To the pump? Of course, and one carried the wiring to the motor, cables waiting to be cut by a junior hacksaw. And the other? Well, this was a pretty old-fashioned installation, so the other probably carried ammonia, and ammonia was lethal.

Jimmy examined the pipes. Identical pipes. He touched them. Cold pipes, equally cold. He placed the tip of his screwdriver on each in turn and put his ear to the handle. Each vibrated in sympathy with the pump. He gazed intently at them to force his senses beyond the opaque casings, but there was no way of knowing, no way other than by blind choice. He backed a yard or two till their entire length was within his field of vision. They were held in position by three saddles.

"There is a moment of crisis..."

Three saddles. Three points of contact with the wall.

A moment lurking round the corner of a summer day on Lewis.

A point of contact with him. The middle saddle moved down from the wall, became a tall man in a white robe who held before him a large book, the open pages of which were covered with writing in a large, spidery hand.

"All moments", Jimmy read, "are moments of crisis. Each one contains meaning, and it is the meaning of life. If you are careless, if you allow your attention to wander, you may miss the one supreme moment, the shattering moment of enlightenment by which you will understand, not perhaps life, or the universe, or infinity, but that these are understandable.

Your moment is there among all the moments. You will see it as a finger pointing, and you will know."

Jimmy looked up at the tiled wall, bare but for the two parallel pipes that ran its entire length and were saddled at three points. His fingers were numb with cold as he wrapped his handkerchief round the handle of his hacksaw. He advanced to the wall, grasped the top pipe, and began to cut.

# Whom Once the People Loved

From a deep pool of misery Agnosticus considered the stranger's question. He turned a lifeless eye towards the thronged street and answered in a voice that held the despair which lies beyond anger. "The procession is what you can see: a gathering of gutter filth, a superstitious mob dazzled by a flame and bent on quenching it with dirt."

The stranger gave him an amused glance. "I take it you are not in sympathy with the local form of religious expression."

Agnosticus looked at the tall, brown-robed figure as though seeing him for the first time. "You take it right."

A great cry from the crowds lining the route swung their attention back to the street. Into view came a large, ceremonial litter carried on the naked shoulders of a score of men. The centre of the bare, polished platform was occupied by an ornate throne in gilt and crimson. On the throne sat an old man. Long, richly-decorated robes of purple and gold flowed from shoulder to foot. His white head was bare but for a narrow circlet of small green leaves. He leaned back in the chair, his eyes closed, his long grey beard contrasting the purple of his chest.

"Hail, Barabbas!" the mob chanted. "Hail Joshua Barabbas!" And they bowed their obeisances.

The old man gave no sign. He sat, motionless but for the sway of the litter, as though in some sad world of his own. The mob's chant became a scream. Agnosticus swore and threw his hand to the hilt of his short broadsword. The stranger's fingers clamped round his wrist.

"Steady, soldier!" The voice was even, the eyes clear and gentle as they scanned the angry face. "The sword is out of place here, my friend. You are one among a multitude."

For a long moment the two men stared at each other, then Agnosticus capitulated.

"You're right", he sighed, and pushed the sword back into its scabbard. "I can hardly keep my hands off this scum. They're not fit to tie his sandals." He gazed venomously after the crowd that had fallen in behind the procession as it moved towards the outskirts of the town.

"Perhaps," the stranger said, stroking his short black beard thoughtfully, "perhaps you will explain to me the meaning of these festivities. They appear to be harmless enough."

"Harmless?" Agnosticus echoed. "Is sanctified murder harmless?" He hitched up his short kilt in a characteristic gesture. "I've seen fighting all round the Empire these twenty years. I could drink blood and think nothing of it. In this little army of occupation alone, I've seen enough murder and rape to put callouses on my very soul. But I tell you, this day's work will come between me and my sleep forever. Explain it? I'll tell you the story, for I know it better than most, but I'll not explain it. There's no explanation, just as there's no justice. Gods and men alike are guttersnipes and there's no point to a civilisation that must kiss the arse of barbarism."

Agnosticus stopped and looked suspiciously at the stranger. "You think I exaggerate? Oh, I know!" He dismissed impatiently the stranger's disclaimer. Then his eyes grew tender. "He taught me the simplicity of truth, and the real dignity of man. He gave me a dream to hold, a dream of reality, and for that he is to die."

"He is to die?" The stranger was puzzled. "You mean the old man on the litter: But he is of high rank, is he not?"

"High rank indeed. He has been king all day. Didn't you hear them cry 'Barabbas' at him? That means Son of the Father. This morning they made him the son of their God. Before nightfall they'll sacrifice him." He took a step in the direction taken by the crowd and signalled his companion to join him. "If you like I'll tell you the story as we go along. We might as well see it through." He moved off with his soldier's stride, and the stranger fell into step beside him, There was silence between them for a while as Agnosticus collected his thoughts.

"I first heard of him", he began, "from an old preacher when I was stationed up north. He and I used to argue about theology and the like, and when he heard I was posted here during The Rising, he asked me to visit his old friend, Joshua Ben Pandira. 'He has some ideas that will interest you greatly', he told me. I promised to pay my respects if it was possible, but it was some time before I was able to carry out my promise. There were a number of hotheads to clean up here, and for a while we had a no-fraternisation order. Things did ultimately quieten down, and I found myself with little to do. I never was one to take much pleasure in barrack-room conversation, so, remembering my promise, I made enquiries about Joshua Ben Pandira, and discovered his house in the poorer quarter of the town.

"I remember vividly my first sight of him. He sat cross-legged on a mat on the floor with a group of men forming a semicircle in front of him. The light from a single lamp flickered on his face as he talked. So intent was the group on the old man's words that my entry went unnoticed, so I sat down quietly by the door and listened.

"Soon, I too was under the spell of his soft old voice. He spoke about love, the love of man for his brother man – and he was not talking about the Greek Disease – and about responsibility. There was not a man in the room but hung on his every word. 'Remember,' he said, 'you are responsible for your thoughts and your deeds, not to a God, not to a Devil, not to any man, but to yourself. By your motives, you make yourself what you are, and when you are stripped naked of the flesh that covers you, you will be seen and known in truth for the thing you have made of yourself.'

"That was the first of my many visits. I came to know and love him like a father. He never spoke of himself, but, through his other disciples, I learnt something of his background. He was not merely a teacher. He carried into his own life all the things he taught. The brotherhood of man to him was a reality to be practised every day of his life. Personal responsibility was the mainspring of his existence. He bent the knee to no God but the divinity in man. He was poor and lived a simple, gentle life. Always he helped those around him; always he taught what he lived and knew to be right. The poor brought him their problems and he went to any lengths to help in their solution. He was regarded by many as a saint, and this saddened him. 'I am no more than a man like the rest of you', he claimed; but there were many who held him in awe.

"He was too good for this world, and he was upsetting forces that were too powerful. The priests took a hand. He was an atheist, and a dangerous one. He spread his atheism like a plague. Spies were set on him and his words reported. Albinus, our much-respected and lily-livered Procurator, was approached and supplied with evidence that a certain Joshua Ben Pandira was inciting young men to rebellion against the Imperial Authority. I received wind of this move and begged him to go into hiding. He smiled at me. 'What dark cavern would you have me occupy, my son?' he said. 'The seeds I sow thrive only in the sunlight.'

"He knew the danger, and carried on with his life as though nothing had altered. He was arrested and condemned to death after a mockery of a trial. I offered myself as a witness in his defence and was told bluntly by my superiors to mind my own business. You would have thought an execution would satisfy them, but the priests were not finished with him yet. A rebel's death was too clean for his like. He had yet to pay the price of his heresy. So they dug into the barbarous beginnings of their tribe.

"Long ago, the king was regarded as the son of God. At a time of national peril, it was the custom to sacrifice him in the hope that God would accept the life of his earthly son in exchange for the wellbeing of his people. Later, when kings became more powerful, it was usual to substitute a representative of the king; and later still, with the enlightenment of the barbarians, a condemned murderer was released and hailed as King-for-a-day, before being slain as a living sacrifice.

"Old superstitions die hard, particularly when they are encouraged by a crafty priesthood with a vested interest in ignorance. A word in the Procurator's ear, that the people might be less restive if treated to one of the old religious spectacles, persuaded the worthy Albinus to take a convenient holiday. These things can be arranged without fuss. There has been feasting all day today. The people have been acclaiming their king, Joshua Barabbas, Joshua, son of the Father."

Agnosticus finished his narrative with a break in his voice. The two men walked on until they topped a slight rise just beyond the limits of the town. Beneath them thronged the mass of people. Ahead of the crowd, lashed halfway up the knotted trunk of a large tree, hung the emaciated body of the old man. The robes had been removed, and on the naked belly spread a great red stain. As they watched, the first stone was cast. It thudded against the old man's flesh and rebounded to he turf. The stranger muttered something in a tongue Agnosticus did not understand. "What did you say?" he asked.

"There is, in my land," the stranger replied, "an old poem

which translates something like:

> Whom once the people loved,
> They came to worship;
> Whom they worshipped, feared,
> And whom they feared, destroyed.

Tears glistened in his eyes and rolled slowly down his cheek as he spoke. His face took on a look of agony, of compassion. Agnosticus followed his gaze and saw, with astonishment, that he looked not at the body of the old man, but at the people throwing stones.

# Tents in Haran

The reckoning would come in the morning. It could be dealt with if the night went well, and the night lay with Leah.

Laban looked with satisfaction at the men round the fire. It was a good feast and he took pride in the arrangements. The lands around had been scoured for the choicest fruits. For days the women had been baking their corn pastries and cooking venison, mutton, and goat's flesh, and the wineskins, plentiful and well-filled had been stored a long time in a cool place. Not every day did a daughter of Laban marry.

The men, already well on in wine, were becoming recklessly merry. The lonely songs of shepherd and husbandman gave way to drinking songs and songs of courtship and fecundity. All was noise, the sound of happy singing and laughter.

Laban smiled to himself until his appraising eye rested on Jacob, his nephew and son-in-law-to-be. The boy's wedding garments sat well on him; but he was too silent for the gathering. A queer lad. He was not popular with the men, a stranger even after seven years. He was a good worker, though, and he would prosper. Laban had an eye for a man. That was partly why he had taken this step. His sister, Rebekah, the boy's mother, would approve. But Jacob was too silent in the midst of all this gaiety. Dreaming his dreams again. Too often the wineskin was passing him untouched. Tonight he would be better a little drunk, for suspicion leaves the mind when the wine fume enters. "Come on, Jacob, my son!" Laban cried loudly. "Drink deep, this night is yours."

Jacob started and a slow flush deepened the bronze of his skin. The eyes of the men were on him. Lifting a skin, he poured some wine and drank quickly. He was conscious of the bite of it at his throat and the sour aftertaste in his mouth. He poured again and sipped, slowly this time. Laban and the men, he noticed, had turned their attention back to the singing. His mind sideslipped into reverie.

Waiting... for what you don't know, but the strangest thoughts enter your head "...and in thy seed shall all the families of the earth be blessed..." some phrase from a forgotten tale. And still you wait. There is a breathlessness in the air. Something is trembling to happen, something momentous, significant, something that will change your world. There is the need for meaning. So many questions hang in the mind unanswered. Is it now they are to be resolved? You wait, and the time walks past unnoticed. Was it another of your imaginings like so many more as you worked silently in the fields or watched the flocks these seven years? Always dreaming, dreaming of your blind old father and of the Lord God, and of your brother's birthright, dreaming of a stone rolled from a well, and of a kiss and the feel of an eager body against you.

Laban's voice sliced through his mind like the butcher's knife. "Ho, Jacob! You are too pensive for a new husband. Does not even the wine put a curb on your impatience?"

Jacob stretched out an embarrassed hand for the wineskin. Laban allowed the smile to remain on his lips, though his eyes were watchful. It would not take much more to fuddle the boy. He glanced beyond the circle of firelight to the intermittent shadows where the bridal tent stood. A lamp flickered for a moment and was extinguished. A patch of deeper shadow moved away from the tent. Zilpah, the handmaiden, leaving her mistress. Leah then, was perfumed and couched and waiting for her man. Laban nodded to himself, satisfied, and returned his attention to the feast.

Zilpah entered her tent and found Bilhah preparing for bed. "They're still carousing", she said. "It will be a drunken husband for my mistress this night."

"No more than she deserves, that one", Bilhah rejoined. "She's like an old she-goat."

Zilpah turned on her angrily. "You've no right to talk like that", she cried. "She's worth a score of your Rachels."

Bilhah shrugged her naked young shoulders and began combing her hair. "She's not pretty," Zilpah continued, "but she's good and kind and gentle, not like some I could name, always gadding about making eyes at the men."

Bilhah tumbled her long raven hair down her back. "What's left but to be kind when you have a face that men shudder to see?" She gave an undignified snort. "Anyway, she's not so kind either when she can stoop to stealing her sister's husband."

"That's wicked talk, girl", Zilpah cried. "May the Lord God forgive you for it. You know she must obey her father." Zilpah dabbed her eyes with the corner of a face cloth. "When I left her, poor soul, she was weeping for the shame of it."

But Bilhah had abandoned the argument and focused her interest on her lithe brown limbs which she massaged speculatively. "What do you think it is like, Zilpah," she enquired, "when a man comes to your tent?"

"You'll know soon enough, I expect", Zilpah answered sullenly.

Bilhah wasn't listening. "I wish I was lying in wait for him." She ran her hands caressingly over her belly and her thighs. "I could love him", she sighed. "He is so young and lean and strong, and he has such nice words. He could say such beautiful things in the night."

Zilpah laughed in spite of herself and gave Bilhah a friendly slap on the behind. "You will fall with child to your imagination one of these days", she said.

"I believe you have a fancy for him yourself", pouted Bilhah.

"No", Zilpah said soberly. "He's not my meat. He thinks too much. Give me a man with red blood who remembers he is a man, not a saint who dreams he is in heaven and forgets he is in bed." She sat down on her cot and began do disrobe. "Anyway," she concluded, "We are not the only maids in a virgin bed tonight."


Rachel wiped the angry tears from her face. She had a week of it to bear. Then she would show them. She could still hear the men singing their bawdy songs out at the fire. She would show them all. It was she who had conquered him, she whom he loved. It was she who remembered his kiss at the well seven years ago, the hurt of his arms as he pulled the breath from her, and the throb of her blood as his body crushed her breasts.

She had a week of it to bear and then she would laugh at Leah's claim. There was no competition from that one with her old woman's face and her old woman's ways. She had no passion in her and you could never bear sons without passion.

A week of her sister would whet his desire. A week of Leah and he would come, more ardent than ever, to her tent. And she would show them. She would be mistress. Hers would be the sons who would inherit all these lands, for the land would be Jacob's. He could wait. He was above all the others. He knew how to wait. Hadn't he disdained all other women and cut himself off from the men these seven years? He was aloof and apart, like a God. Yet she knew he was passionate. She had seen his eyes when he looked at her and she recalled his kiss at the well. Her body burned when she remembered that kiss.

Tonight he should have been coming to her. She should have lain in the bridal tent, oiled and perfumed and naked, waiting for him to come and claim his right as a man and her lord. Instead it was Leah who waited, Leah who lay, cold and passionless, hiding her ugly face in the darkness of the tent, waiting, waiting for Rachel's man.

But surely he would know. Surely he would feel the difference and know it was not the wife he had waited seven long years for. He must know. He must find out. In anger he would strike Leah to the ground and come storming like thunder to claim his rightful wife. And she would be ready for him. Yes, he would know. Leah would give herself away. She couldn't sustain the deceit, she hadn't the courage. It all depended on Leah.

The singing of the men was muffled and unreal in the bridal tent. Leah, her tender eyes hot and weary, lay staring up into the darkness. How had she supported these last days? She had gone about her work with the other women, cooking, baking, preparing her sister's wedding feast, and all the time, knowing the part she had to play. Tears, agony, the scenes with her father, Rachel's glowering looks, and the constant sense of Jacob's presence, all had oppressed and confused her. She would be forgiven by the Lord God but not by Jacob. Yet it was none of her doing. She loved him, she desired him with all her soul and body, but not this way, not this shameful way.

Leah closed her eyes but she could not shut out the images that rose in front of her. She had watched him during his seven years' stay. She had taken goat's milk to him as he worked in the fields, and watched him drink apart from the other men with his eyes averted. How she had longed to clasp his dark, beautiful head to her breast and smooth away the shy, puzzled frown from his brow, and to kiss the hurt from his eyes. They never understood him, how he kept away from the men and feigned not to notice the women. He was a man in his lean young strength, but a boy also, sensitive, easy to hurt, and often with tears behind his eyes. This she saw, and in her secret dreams he was her son, her husband, her lover.

Now this! She was to destroy him. The thought made her feel sick. She saw vividly his torment when, in the morning, he discovered Leah, the ugly one, in Rachel's bed. She saw him spit out her kisses and rub the feel of her body from his arms. She watched the fire in his eyes, the inner vision that sustained him, fade and die. She would have her night of happiness and shame, of passion and grief, and she would destroy utterly the one she loved above all.

Outside, the feast was breaking up. Men were drifting away, singing, to their distant tents. Coarse voices shouted their lecherous goodnights. Then she heard footsteps approaching the bridal tent. He was coming. She clenched her fists until the nails hurt her palms, and silently she prayed.

Jacob fumbled with the flap of the tent and hiccupped as the wine caught his breath.

# The Rabbit

The Ancient Warrior complained twice about the heat before Mrs Bollinger paused in her knitting and leaned towards her husband. "Give Mr MacIvor a glass of beer, Henry."

Henry Bollinger returned abruptly from some far country. "Beer? Oh yes, sorry. You'll have a drink, Mac?" He disappeared into the kitchen and returned shortly, his arms laden with bottled beer and clean tumblers.

Old MacIvor accepted the drink graciously and caressed the glass with a blue-veined hand. He examined the head critically. "Sticks to the glass", he commented. "Always tell a good brew if it sticks to the glass right the way down." He prepared his nicotined moustache for action, semaphored a "Good health" in the general direction of Mrs Bollinger, and drank expertly.

His drinking technique was a matter of supple wrist-work. The militarily-trimmed head remained perpendicular as though supporting a bearskin. Only the glass tilted, tilted and was smoothly drained. With the precision of a royal salute the old man wiped his moustache, brought the glass to attention on a spot on the table where it could conveniently be refilled, and clamped an evilly mature pipe between his few sentinel front teeth. "See Pringle got life", he headlined.

Bollinger paused in the act of pouring another drink. "Yes," he said slowly, "I've seen the paper."

"A bad lot", MacIvor continued as though Henry had not spoken. "We should have hanging for his like. Or the triangle. Or lash 'em to the wheel of a gun. That'd fix a lot of them."

"What a bloodthirsty old villain you are." Mrs Bollinger's voice came over the click of her needles without interrupting it.

"Bloodthirsty?" The Ancient Warrior sounded a little shocked. His pale eyes looked reproachfully at his hostess. "I've been a fighting man most of my life, Mrs B, but I don't think anyone could call me bloodthirsty." He bayonetted the air with the stem of his pipe and leaned forward. "I'll tell you this though. I've

65

come up against a few Pringles in my time and I've learned there's only one way to deal with them. Hit them hard and hit them often and don't stop until you don't have to hit them any more." He lifted the replenished glass and eyed it judicially.

Henry stood at the open window and looked out at the road. Nothing moved in the hot, dry air. Under the leaden sky the asphalt was grey and uninviting. "There's a storm coming", he said, half to himself.

His wife shot him a quick glance, her forehead almost imperceptibly furrowed. The needles continued to weave and click.

MacIvor completed his manoeuvres with the second empty glass. "Don't know what the country's coming to", he complained. "What with football casuals and Stanley knives and machetes... Pah!" His gesture consigned a generation to the firing squad.

Mrs Bollinger knitted deftly and the little frown remained to corrugate her brow. Henry turned aimlessly from the window and wiped his face with the back of his hand. "God, but it's hot tonight." He caught his wife's eye and looked away. "Think the kids will be all right?"

She nodded. "They were asleep when I looked in."

Henry intercepted the Warrior's reflective look towards the empty glass and picked up another bottle. "Drink up while you can, Mac, we live in a most violent age."

Mac considered for a moment as the liquid gurgled into the glass. "Maybe it is", he agreed. "Maybe it is that kind of age, but at least you were never a man of violence."

Henry watched, fascinated, the old soldier's drinking performance. "You're wrong you know, Mac. I'm full of violence. We all are. That's why life in these civilised times is so complicated."

"I don't follow you."

Henry leaned his elbows on his knees. "It's like this, Mac. The primitive part of me loves a fight, a real fight complete with blood and spilled brains and so on, but the veneer of civilisation makes me ashamed of that love, and the clash between the two produces fear. So here I am, going about spoiling for battle, hating myself for it, and living in abject terror lest the wrong side of me should win."

"Tripe!" said the Ancient Warrior.

"Mac!" sighed Henry. "You're probably right."

With old MacIvor gone and the empty bottles cleared away the Bollingers sat in the gloaming, one each side of the unlit fire. The heat enclosed them, hung around them like some ponderous curtain, and rendered almost tangible the click of the knitting needles. The only other sounds were those far-off ones of the falling day. Henry held a book open on his knees. He was not reading.

When the shadows in the room were so long that the movements of his wife's hands were barely discernible Henry closed his book quietly and placed it on the occasional table. He rose and glanced across the fireplace. The needles faltered in their dance, stopped for a moment, then picked up and sped on. Henry turned, his shoulders hunched, and paced slowly through the kitchen and out of the back door. Avoiding the small rabbit-hutch against the wall, he crossed the path to the toolshed and lifted a spade.

The hole he dug was small and roughly rectangular. It took longer to dig than was strictly necessary. A few inches beneath the surface he struck a good-sized stone and it was several minutes before he cleared it to the edge. When the digging was done he leaned on the spade and wiped his face. Away on the horizon lightning flickered.

The rabbit hutch was in the deeper shadow of the wall. Henry removed the wire mesh and fumbled in his pocket for a match. By its bright flare he made out the familiar, childish script above the flap. "Peter's House." He looked inside.

The small white figure was huddled in a corner. For a few moments the match's flame was reflected from dull pink-rimmed eyes. During those seconds Henry saw only the damaged hind feet, the skin rotted away, the bones showing, mauve and glistening.

With gentle, clumsy hands he withdrew the creature from its box and held it, swaying, by the ears. He touched its neck with the outside edge of his right hand which he then drew away in a slow upward curve. The beast was a grey blob in the darkness of the wall. Henry stayed his hand at its zenith and slowly let it fall to his side. He took his handkerchief from his pocket and wrapped it carefully round the mutilated hind feet. No sound or struggle came from the animal. Henry closed his fingers round the handkerchief and, holding the limp bundle firmly, head downwards, he walked across the garden.

He straddled the hole and bent his knees so that the rabbit was poised over the stone. He raised his arm, then lowered it again and planted his feet more firmly. He took a deep breath. Once more his arm rose, paused, then thudded down upon the stone. Once, twice, three times, in a frenzy of movement, the arm rose and fell, rose and fell. At last he released his hold and the little white body fell into the hole and remained quite still.

Hastily kicking the stone into the grave Henry shovelled the earth on top of it and packed it down tight with his feet. Lightning flashed again in the distance as he returned the spade to the tool shed. He re-entered the kitchen. On his way to the sink he paused and listened at the living-room door. It was pure fancy, of course, but the click of the knitting needles made him think of teardrops.

# Procon

Shulman's question hangs between us in the night mountain air. What can I say more than I have already said, that Procon is the most efficient machine in the complex?

"What is so wonderful about efficiency?"

How can I answer such a question? How can I express what Procon means to me? Can I tell him of wonder, of awe; can I explain affection for a machine?

"It never fails." I say it, but I know it is an inadequate thing to say. "It never fails."

"It would be a sorry world that had no failures." A sorry world, he says. "Is that not a fault in us? We turn our backs on failures. We refuse to see them, and a benign regime accommodates our myopia. Failures are expunged."

Expunged!

I think I am a failure. But not to Procon. I feed her information on laser disk and watch her digestion on the VDUs. I coax her, adjust her, nurse her like a child, and in return she responds to my every move. She is Procon. She runs the factory.

Procon never fails. How can I make him see? It is life and love, the dignity of labour, the achievement of scientific endeavour. It is Procon, my machine. It is faith and confidence and peace. It is all the things I do not know with Tana.

Tana had bathed and put on her blue dress, the one that told you about her body, her magnificent body. When I left, she was combing down her long, tawny hair.

I know of passion and suspicion, the cry of blood and the whimper of fear. I know the pride of possession and the dread of loss. Procon gives me all; Tana gives her body.

Schulman pursues a thing. Perhaps he senses. "You have made a God of your machine. You should ask yourself what need in you demands such idolatry?"

Am I conscious of need? I am aware of contentment when I am on shift with Procon. Peace at other times depends on Tana, and sometimes on the mountains. The mountains have the moon in them, and the moon leaves mysterious dark places. They brood.

I wonder where Schulman comes from. Somewhere up here, I suppose. You meet him suddenly on the pass or up one of the gullies. He is an archaic figure, white-haired and bearded – anarchic. He talks blasphemy and treason with a disturbingly logical air. But always he is ancient, ageless, like some patriarch from the old myths. This talk of making a God of my machine; Gods went out with the Lefties who fled northwards over the border so long ago.

"Your machine is your refuge and your strength." This in his patriarchal tone. "Refuge from what, I wonder."

I don't like the way Ring looks at Tana, and I don't like the way Tana answers the look.

"You have to be careful how you treat the Block Warden", she says. "He can make things difficult."

But I don't like Ring. I don't like his arrogance, and the way he strips Tana with his eyes. I don't like the grin he gives me as I pass his office on my way out to nightshift. I am too often on nightshift. I don't like Ring.

There is no peace with Tana. There is too much of her that is not mine. Even in loving there is that fierce hunger of hers, and the feeling, the dread, that I have been inadequate. Then the traitor thought comes: I am not loved. I am used, and I am not… efficient.

Procon is efficient, and I am the guard of its efficiency.

"Your refuge and your strength", Schulman said. My refuge and my strength.

"You are all enslaved by your own desire for power." Schulman is developing another theme.

"The regime has power over the people, the factory managers over the workers, the block wardens over the workers' families, and you over your machine."

I over my machine. Yes, I suppose, in a way, it is a feeling of power, of orders transmitted and obeyed implicitly.

"But you are all slaves. You must feed and tend and nurse the children you control or the source of your power disappears. It's like this because of the sense of God-like power it gives you. You press a button, it reacts in the way you planned. You feed in your orders, it dances to your music, and how big you feel, and how clever. But think of the years you have spent serving it, coaxing it, feeding it world without end, and how big are you? How clever are you, the handmaiden of a few tonnes of metal and ceramic and a few kilometres of wire?"

Schulman pauses, but he doesn't glance at the shadows, as I do.

"Oh yes! I'll grant it dances very prettily when you perform your mysterious, technological rites, but it is no less a puppet on your string than you are on theirs. And to what end? To give a sense of power? To satisfy a craving for bigness? To cover the reality of your own insignificance?

"It is useless. When you take a slave, you chain yourself to him. In the long run, the puppet calls the tune."

It is blasphemy to speak this way, and treason to listen and not report. But in the mountains there is no one to hear. The shadows are rock folds and are empty. In town it is different. There, every window is an eye, and round every corner there is an ear. THEY are everywhere. THEY know everything. The factory managers would report. The block wardens would report.

But the block warden is not in the mountains. Here among the dark places left by the moon there is only the strange old man with the white hair and beard and the sad, screwed-up eyes. And he talks in his dry, old-man's voice, of wild, dangerous, treasonable things, that excite, because it is wrong to listen to them and not report. But there is no one in the shadowy places to hear them and tell.

Ring is back at his post in the block, watching and listening. I passed him as I came out and he stopped me.

"Going out on your own, Greig?"

"Yes."

"Up the pass?"

"Yes."

He put a light to his cigarette, cupping the flame in his great paws. The thick, reddish hair came down over the wrists. His brown, appraising eyes never wavered.

"Tana going out?"

"No... a bit of a headache."

I felt his eyes on my back as I walked across the courtyard.

"The lust for power," Schulman is saying, "is self-corrosive."

Tana had bathed and put on her blue dress. It accentuated her breasts and showed the shape of her thighs when she moved.

She began to do things with her hair. "Sunday", she explained.

I have a sudden impulse to tell Schulman about Tana. Sickeningly, I can see two great hands with the thick, reddish hair down over the wrists, two great, red hands and a blue dress shaped by the thigh, two hands fumbling... fumbling.

But there is no need to tell Schulman about Tana and Procon, about being and not being, about loving and fearing, about torment and peace.

No! There is no need to tell Schulman about Tana and Procon.

# A Queen on a White Horse

When old McCance died Devlin staked his claim.

"Don't forget now," he told Sister Tannahill, "I want that window before you bring anybody else in here."

"All right, Mr. Devlin", Sister humoured him. "Nurse will move your bed as soon as she has a minute."

She bustled out of the two-man side-room into the main passage. Old men were the limit, she thought, pathetic maybe, but at times positively ghoulish. Her instructions to the staff nurse were brief. Mr. Devlin's bed was to be moved over beside the window, and Mr. Kirk brought from the ward to fill the vacant space.

McCance's death, part of the routine present, slipped imperceptibly into the routine past, and was cancelled by clean linen. He was killed by age and disease, depersonalised by medical detachment, and, finally, erased by statistics. But he had occupied a space in the little room, had described a world outside the window, and had stood between Devlin and the coveted view of it. Devlin remembered him.

There was McCance's individual and rather high-flown way of saying things:

"Meadows, square, verdant and cared for. Pine woods, dark and mysterious."

It reminded him of the way QM people described everything in the army:

"Caps, Field Service, other ranks for the use of.

"Bottles, water.

"Bottles, urine, male patients for the convenience of.

"Nurse!" He bellowed.

The window had become an obsession. It seemed to symbolise his irritation with life, his age, his illness, his sense of imprisonment within the sluggish body and his preoccupation with its functions. He was incensed that McCance, propped up with pillows, could see out into the world beyond, while he was condemned to look at the plaster-board ceiling, or count the saddles that clamped the electrical conduit to the green and buff walls. He continually pestered the other for descriptions of the view and commentaries on the life outside. But it tended to be a frustrating occupation, for as often as not, McCance was too ill or too deeply sedated to co-operate.

There were times, though, when the emaciated face achieved mobility, the thin lips beneath the yellow moustache humorously twitched, and the dark, sunken eyes flashed an almost gay intelligence. On such occasions he would answer Devlin's questions at length, the articulate speech thickened with phlegm, until the words became attenuated by weariness, and the eyelids were pulled shut by the weight of the drugs.

"Shadows, long over the lea... a glint of setting sun on the wet slates of the distant steeple."

"Anybody there?"

"No. No." An old head shaking and a half-smile. "No contentious human to mar the peace of a westering world, and it is the wrong time of day for the horsewoman on the edge of the forest."

The eyes and the mouth together gave a swift, baffling impression of mockery before they dissolved in sleep. Devlin growled impatiently to himself and fell to thinking about the girl on the horse.

Every morning, it seemed, if the weather was right, she came riding slowly up the path at the edge of the wood. McCance's portrayal of her had been brittle, intermittent, contingent on the weather, his mood and his degree of consciousness.

"A youthful female on a white horse... flecks of colour against the dark pines... brown breeches, red sweater, yellow hair to the shoulder... proud, young, straight, an equestrian Diana..."

It was this picture that Devlin most avidly desired, this description, more than any other, that concentrated his greed for the bed by the window, and his envy of its occupant. In his mind the scene was glinting light slashed across green, rolling fields to the black mystery of the forest's rim. She rode the path on her chalk-white steed like a queen, and she was the magic of it all. She was the magic of it all, and she belonged to him, They rode the path together and surveyed the broad, green shires. Leather creaked, sun glistened on the flanks of the animals, leg brushed on leg, and his heart leapt, and his hand stretched out seeking

74

hers. He was young and in love with his young queen. The world was young and in love with the sun. Magic... Magic... The shimmer of it... The phantom shimmer of it...

And there was the drab fantasy of the real world, the world of bedclothes, bedpans, bedsores, the world of the sports page and the war in the Middle East, the world of plasterboard and conduit. And there was pain, and being sick, and having everything done for you. You lay there festering in your own corruption and you questioned the life out of old McCance. You hated him because he was dying and because he talked better than you and because he had the bed by the window. You hated him because it was only through his eyes you saw the green, glinting world of your young queen. You wished him dead.

Well, he was dead.

Devlin, propped up with pillows, lay locked in his pain and stared out of the window. Kirk, tired of plasterboard, addressed himself across the room.

"What's it like?"

"What?"

"The view. What's the view like?"

"Oh, the view." Devlin looked at him searchingly for a moment. "Well, you know, fields, hedges, a bit of a wood." His lip twisted slightly as though with pain.

"Every morning," he said, "when the weather's fine, a young girl on a horse comes riding up the path at the edge of the trees."

His eyes wandered slowly over the blank facade of the grey brick wall that blocked all view from the window except for a little segment of sky.

"It's a white horse", he said.

# A Long Line of Spinsters

I had known Caroline precisely two weeks when she seduced me. Those fantastic days when the war was fizzling out hold more fantasy for me than for most. There was something of the witch about Caroline.

The bar parlour of the Three Bells in York that afternoon merely added to my depression. Solitary drinking is bad for a man at any time, but for a man suffering a too-long and too-close acquaintanceship with heavy bombers, it was soul-destroying. The bleached drab serving at the bar, with her "Yes ducks, no ducks, don't mind if I do ducks" was getting on my nerves. Some Canadian types were shooting the old lines to a couple of bored prostitutes in one corner. Half a dozen of the local scroungers were noisily slinging darts for pints. I was slowly getting murderously drunk.

Suddenly I had had enough. My beer only half-finished, I rose, jammed on my cap, field service, and stumbled through the swing door into the cold March day. There was only one place for me to go. For all my agnosticism I was a frequent visitor at the Minster. The Zouche Chapel, a small sanctuary set aside for private prayer, seemed to have the power to dissolve my fits of depression. It had an atmosphere, a something that soothed my spirit, restored my faith in myself. "Pilgrimage to Mecca", I thought.

The organist was practising Bach as I entered the Cathedral. A good sign. I was into Baroque at that time. I made my way to the small oak door that leads to the Chapel, entered and closed the door quietly behind me. The three inches of ancient timber reduced Bach to that mysterious level that makes shivers dance up and down the spine. Already the magic of the place was on me, yet I knew it was no more than a small, rectangular room with a vaulted ceiling, a few rows of cane-bottomed chairs and, on a raised dais at one end, a little altar. In front of the dais a woman stood. I felt a momentary irritation. She was trespassing.

This was my property. Then she turned.

Light through the stained glass shimmered on the burnished bronze stream that cascaded round her head and over her shoulders. I had a sudden dazzling impression of enormous brown eyes gazing steadily at me from a serene, oval face. An elusive half-smile played on the full, red lips. She was tall for a woman and wore... clothes, I suppose. I didn't notice. The light encircled her head like a halo, appropriately, I remember thinking. Our eyes met and held for a century or two. Doubt and fear were resolved. I felt the spell of the place, the half-muted Bach, the Chapel and this angel. My depression escaped in a long sigh.

She spoke. "It is peaceful, isn't it?"

"The peace that passeth all understanding", I said. Then, afraid her smile might be slightly mocking, "A clerical cliché, I know, but there really is something about this place."

"I understand", she said, and by the way she said it I knew she did understand.

"I'm Danny."

"I'm Caroline." We laughed, and talking was easy as we walked side by side out of the Cathedral.

The bus back to camp that night had its usual complement of drunken airmen. I was happily oblivious of the noise. My thoughts were on Caroline. She was entrancing, beautiful, self-reliant, individual, remarkably intelligent. We had discussed philosophy and religion. We had professed iconoclasm, dethroned the gods, and invested human beings with responsibility. We had sipped gin, and talked our way to the door of her flat. We had promised to meet again, and she had allowed me to kiss her good night. I was bomb-happy.

During the next two weeks I feasted. Duty was a long, dragging interval between meetings with Caroline. Those meetings were a joy. All the way around the City Wall we argued about Freud. At Bishopgate I put my hand on her elbow and said, "I love you, Caroline."

"That proves my point", she rejoined.

Over pint tankards at the Coach and Horses we agreed on the *Higher Criticism*. I was amazed at her knowledge. She had read Volney and Dupuis in the original French, and could quote J M Robertson backwards. During a modern waltz she defended Picasso against my case for Impressionism. Her political mentor was Shaw, as indeed he was mine, but she had waded through the Webbs' massive work on Trades Unions while I had contented myself with *The Intelligent Woman's Guide to Socialism.* And yet she had nothing about her of the traditional bluestocking. She was fresh and sparkling and stimulating, and she was lovely and wise, and I was madly in love with her.

We sat in her flat one evening enjoying a last drink before I caught my bus.

"I start seven days leave tomorrow, Caroline."

"Going home, Danny?"

"No. I thought of booking a room at the George for the week so that I can see you every day."

She smiled, but made no comment. I put down my glass and leaned forward. "Caroline," I said gently, "I know I appear to be rushing things, but these two weeks have been the happiest I have ever known." I took her hands. "Caroline, dearest, I love you, and I want to marry you."

There was a long silence. I gazed anxiously at her face. She looked steadily at me and the elusive half-smile played about her lips. Her fingers tightened on mine and I held my breath. Then suddenly her breath relaxed and I knew she had come to a decision.

"No, Danny", she said. "I won't marry you. But I want you to spend your leave here with me. I want to have a child."

Seconds passed before I fully realised the import of her quiet, matter-of-fact statement. My face must have shown some of the confusion in my mind, for she smiled kindly and said, "Don't look so shocked, Danny. It's really quite simple, and surely not unflattering?"

"But Caroline…"

"Don't ask questions, dear", she interrupted. "Not just now." She leaned closer and put her hands on my shoulders. "Look at me, Danny." I looked into her large eyes and my pulses raced. "Poor Danny! You are just a wee bit conventional about the protocol of seduction. Why don't you let your feelings dictate the ground rules? Relax and enjoy." I relaxed and drew her against me. "Your bus, Danny."

"To hell with my bus", and I let my feelings dictate.

The week that followed was a sort of Paradise. I lived and loved furiously with hardly a thought but for the moment. Each day was a wondrous adventure, each night a consummation. We lived at high pressure and I allowed myself no time to heed the puzzled ache within me. At that stage I was too grateful for having Caroline so completely to myself to worry over the impermanence of the arrangement. I felt she would explain in her own time. So I respected her silence and put hope and despair on hold.

My leave came to an end. The war intruded as it always did. On my last evening we sat together in the flat. I was packed and ready to go.

"Drink, Danny?"

"Gin please." I watched the movements of her body as she crossed to the sideboard. "I still want to marry you, Caroline."

She poured gin into two glasses and handed one to me. "I know you do, my dear. But I won't let you."

"But if you should have a child... "

"I will have a child." There was a strange sort of resolute pride in her voice.

"Please, Caroline, I don't understand."

She was silent and thoughtful for a moment, then she looked at me squarely and said, "I will try to explain, Danny, you might understand." She paused, searching for the right words. "It all springs from my history, the history of my family. It is my destiny."

"Destiny?" I was puzzled. Fatalism hardly squared with what I knew of her philosophy.

"Not the blind destiny of Karma", she continued. "I mean that my life is preordained by an effort of will. My will."

"It began with my great-grandmother. Hers was the hackneyed story of the lady's maid seduced by the husband of her mistress. When it became obvious she was pregnant she was dismissed. The man made no attempt to help her and pride kept her silent. Life in those days was hard on a woman in her situation. But nobody ever knew what cruelties she endured. She was a woman of spirit and character. She bore her daughter, scraped money enough to start a dressmaking business, and laid the foundations of a fortune.

"And she did more. She founded a dynasty, a dynasty of Matriarchs. 'No man shall ever head my family', she said. 'Though it makes bastards of us all, we shall be free of the chains that bind women to men. Our women will find their own feet, and force their own terms on life.'" Caroline paused. Her eyes shone, her head was thrown back. I remained silent, watchful, fearful of breaking the spell. She spoke again, more quietly. "Marriage is out, Danny. Grandmother was a bastard, so was Mother, so am I." She laughed. "We are a long line of spinsters."

A thought struck me. "What if you should have a son, Caroline?"

"Such things happen of course. Grandmother was unfortunate. She had two sons before Mother was born. The boys are well enough brought up, but their place is that occupied by daughters in ordinary homes."

"And the fathers?" I asked.

"There are no fathers."

"But what if one should claim his child?" I insisted.

"What chance would he have when the mother doesn't know for certain who the father is?" She said this with the old half-smile elusive on her lips. I looked at her for a long time. I could feel the prickle of tears behind my eyes. I rose hopelessly to my feet.

"Goodbye, Caroline."

"Goodbye, Danny."

I picked up my bag and my cap, field service, and went out into the night.

# Cold Crossing

The moon has a slice off her left shoulder. Below her and to the right a bright star points.

Where is the significance to an electronics engineer of the moon having a slice off her left shoulder and a bright star pointing upwards to her right buttock?

I am cold and hungry.

The dark November clouds that merge with the unseen mountains and the twinkling shoreline gave us rain during the day. Above my little portion of the Firth the sky is a clear canvas. The moon and the star are painted there.

If the loudspeaker had only had twenty nuts instead of twenty-four I would have been on the last Gourock boat. Four nuts, and they cost me an hour and headed me for Wemyss Bay.

The water looks slimy, a writhing pit of snakes. Strange what the moon does to water, or water does to the moon.

Electronic bells! It is said that the man who works has a constant companion. It isn't true. All afternoon I was lonely. I was alone in the loft of the bell-tower, alone with the sullen, voiceless loudspeaker. The loudspeaker! A misnomer, a mockery. Nothing was ever more quiet. It hung twenty feet up the tubular scaffold and turned with deliberate, electric-powered ferocity. The wide-flared horn, the dust-sheeted cone, the massive cylinder of the magnet were powerful, lustful. Thirty times a minute it showed me its gaping mouth; but it was dumb.

Behind me the paddles thresh frenziedly the surface of the snakepit. I can visualise bits of moonlight flashing off the revolving blades and settling behind the ship into twin streams of frothing, silvered blood. The vibration of the deck is a steady dub-dub-dub-dub. The wind is cold around my head. I can afford a haircut tomorrow, off the overtime.

In front of me, nearer the bows, a man is standing. He is a tall, vague shape in a light raincoat and a dark hat. The hat doesn't mean anything somehow. It is an irrelevant arrangement of stiff

81

cloth. No meaning. He doesn't move.

It all suddenly crystallises. The aloneness... This is it. It had to come, here or in the bell-tower or in the workshop or at home, terracing, cinema or pub. It chose its place and its circumstance, or I chose. Here it is, here on the Firth somewhere between Dunoon and Innellan beneath a deformed moon and a single signposting star, the sense, the tremendous, desperate, paralysing sense of my existence.

Everything has pointed to this moment. All roads have led to it. I should have known. I did know. I knew and I fought against knowing. I was alone in the tower and I refused to be alone. I fought, you see. I spoke to the bell. The man who works has a constant companion. I spoke to the bell.

"Dumb", I said. "Swing, swing, swing, but dumb as Hell."

I had to go up the scaffold with the meter. Test the feed. Test the brushes. Test the slip-rings. Audio volts at the transformer secondary. Speech coil must be fractured. Right at the heart of things, right at the core of the cone, the cone's core. Little coil fractured at the core of the cone. Little coil at the cone's core.

"You gotta come down, Baby. Holy Gees! You gotta come down."

Eighty pounds of clumsy steel alone with me in the tower and the organist practising below in the church. Twenty pounds of flared horn unbolted and shouldered down the scaffold. That's Bach, the Toccata and Fugue. Heaven in an empty church with the Diapason stopped and the swell box open. Hell is above in the tower loft. Sixty pounds of delicate steel roped and lowered gently to the floor.

Here on the vibrant deck with the moon and the man and the water snakes the loose ends of my past and my future are integrated into the nauseating certainty of my ever-present existence, my eternal subjectivity.

I must be rational. The moon is objective, an opaque spheroid reflecting light. It is outside me. Isn't it? The man is an existent. Isn't he? He exists apart from my consciousness of him. Or does he?

If he should turn and look at me, if he should stare, I would become an object, I would lose my subjectivity. That's it. They all stare. They all conspire to rob me of my existence, and even I participate in the conspiracy.

There is my own life, my children, my wife. I cower beside

them. I get closer to them, closer, closer. I want to be them. I want them to stare, to objectivise me. They see me as an object, husband and father. But I am not. It is they who are wife and children. I know, yet I want them to stare. I can't stand the responsibility of my own existence.

There is a sudden rush of movement behind. A short, light-haired woman hurries breathlessly towards me.

"Have we passed Dunoon?" Her head is bare, and the moonlight has turned it the colour of ashes.

"Dunoon? Oh yes, we left there ten minutes ago." I turn to her. She may be my escape.

"God!" she says in agitation. "My man'll be waitin' for me. God! I'm daft. Got talkin' doon in the saloon 'na never noticed."

"You can get off at Innellan and take a bus." My spirit sinks as I speak. She is too temporary to be escape. I offer my cigarettes.

"Ta", she says. "God! I need this, I'm aw wasted." She shivers as the wind penetrates her thin black coat.

"Come in here." I indicate the open folds of my own coat and she snuggles gratefully against me as I light the cigarettes. I kiss her full on the mouth. Her lips are cold and lifeless and hold the taste of smoke.

"Romance on board ship", she sniggers.

"We are pulling into Innellan", I say.

"Cheerio, well…" she is gone and I am left with the nightmare and the futility. There is no escape. I have never fully realised, before, the need I have always felt for escape. Even in the tower when I spoke to the bell…

Now it's on the floor, speech coil fractured. That means a new cone. Get the old one off. Twenty-four nuts to remove – thank God it isn't glued – twenty-four nuts and one small spanner, twenty-four nuts to the cone. Now the ring, take off the ring. Cone free. Disconnect the speech coil. Pull the cone away. Damn! Look at the dirt in the gap. Gotta be cleaned. Carbon tetrachloride, a rag, a matchstick to poke out the stubborn grit.

We have a free run now across to Wemyss Bay at right angles to the tide. The water is solid underneath. There is only a shallow top layer of snakes. The man in the light raincoat and the irrelevant hat still has his back to me, still he makes no move. I look at him with bitter hatred. If he should turn and stare… I feel sick.

New cone fitted. Connect coil. Centre up. Fit ring. Now the nuts, twenty-four nuts, twenty-four little hexagonal pieces of brass, twenty-four to the cone.

The man turns. He turns and walks slowly away from his place at the bows. He draws abreast and glances at me.

"Cold crossing", he says.

"Twenty-four nuts to the cone", I babble. "Twenty-four nuts to the cone."

He gazes curiously at me for a second and then passes on. I look at the moon. It is an object, my invention, an opaque spheroid reflecting my light. The star is a tear falling into a universe of nothingness.

# Thirty Trips to the Tour

I awoke with cold rain in my face. The waking was agony. There was a gaping split in my forehead and into it hot sand was being poured. I groaned and gave myself up to pain. Minutes passed. Red fire burned behind my eyelids, my head throbbed, my tongue was swollen, my lips cracked. "What's doing, Skipper?"

No answer came from the clouds that darkened the moon. The only sound was the quiet swish of rain on grass. I struggled to sit up, my hands slipping on the floppy wet silk of the parachute. Confused memories crowded my mind.

I had finished taking down the Group Broadcast and switched back to intercom. A yell came from Red in the rear turret. "Night fighter, seven o'clock! Weave, Skipper, weave for God's sake."

I was mixed up about what followed. Just outside my square of perspex the inner port engine exploded in a great billow of orange flame. My head was driven against the transmitter, and the world blacked out.

Had the crew escaped, I wondered? Somebody must have clipped the 'chute to my chest and bundled me through the hatch – Joe, the Navigator, probably. If there was time for that, surely there was time for them all to bale out. The Skipper would stay with the kite until all had gone. Had he made it? The thought hit me in the stomach. The world seemed safer with the Skipper around. Without him the prospect was bleak. My mind slipped back a few hours.

There had been a noticeable excitement among us when we reached the dispersal point. Ronnie Redman, Sergeant Fitter in charge of J–Johnny, was supervising the removal of engine covers. "Last trip, Skipper?" he asked as we approached.

"Don't say 'last', Ronnie," Skip answered, "call it the thirtieth."

I was happy as I climbed aboard and began my pre-op wireless checks. Twenty-nine sticky trips we had done – the Ruhr, Berlin, all the hot flak spots, and now we were to finish our tour of ops on a nice easy French doodlebug site.

The Halibag is a lovely machine, and old J–Johnny is the best of the bunch. The thunder of four Hercules engines is music when they are controlled by a pilot like the Skipper, and you are on the last trip of your tour, and it is a piece of cake like a doodlebug job. I prepared the set to receive the first of the Group Broadcasts and thought contentedly of the crate of beer we had ordered from the Mess bar. We set course.

I groaned again. It was the nearest I could get to a bitter laugh. I knew my head was about to fall off, but I also knew I had to rouse myself and get moving. Where to I had no idea, nor did I know where I was except that it was somewhere in Northern France. But move I must. The parachute had to be hidden. Jerry would be looking for it in the morning. He might even be looking now. Clumsily I unharnessed and staggered around in no sort of order until I stumbled into some bushes. Under these I stowed the mass of wet silk and covered it as well as I could with leaves and branches. As I finished I became aware of a low rumbling in the distance. Away to my left there was a flickering glow in the sky that moved towards me. A train! The rise in front of me was a railway embankment. I crouched behind the bushes as the rumble grew louder.

This was serious. A railway line would probably mean German patrols, and with a crashed aircraft in the neighbourhood these would be on the lookout for escaping survivors. The train passed with a long rattling roar, and I pressed my face into the soaking grass. Slowly the noise receded into the night and I struggled to my feet.

The intermittent flash of a light caught my eye. It came from up the line in the direction the train had taken. I stood dead still, my heart thumping. There it was again. A torch! A patrol! I panicked, turned and ran stumbling and tripping over rough ground. I imagined I could hear a whole army after me. I ran on and on, forever it seemed. My chest was bursting. The wound in my forehead throbbed. I could feel warm blood trickling down my face. My heart pounded. Dark shapes began to loom out of the night all round me. Trees! Branches tore at my flying jacket and thorns scratched my face and hands. Invisible shadows pulled and jostled me. I tripped and fell, half-rose and fell again, face down, almost gibbering with terror. Any moment I would feel the icy plunge of the bayonet in my back.

I lay sobbing for breath and pressed my face into the cold earth. The reaction came. I was weak and dizzy. I vomited, and began to cry like a child.

"Skipper, oh Skipper", I wept, and as though my call had brought him close, I seemed to see his quiet, confident smile and feel the warm, safe cloak of his presence.

"Stop snivelling, you bloody fool", I told myself and immediately felt calmer. I recovered my breath with my senses. No time for panic, mate. I had to think and move while there was still darkness. I fished out my pocket compass and consulted its luminous dial. I had been running east as far as I could tell, which meant the railway stretched north and south from where I had landed. The best I could think of was to move further east a mile or two from the line then turn north and head for the coast. What I was to do when I reached the sea I didn't stop to consider. It was enough for my morale just then to have an objective. Besides, there was, at the back of my mind, a grave doubt of my fitness to get very far.

God knows I was in no shape for route-marching, but I forced myself on into the night. The rain had stopped, but the light of the moon was still filtered by low cloud. I avoided roads, stuck to fields and used the cover of hedges and trees. Walking was difficult, for the ground was soft and muddy and my flying boots grew heavier with every step. My head troubled me, my tongue felt swollen, my mouth was dry like paper. A drink would have been nice, but, although I clambered in and out of every ditch, I found no stream that would quench my thirst, no puddle that would ease my head.

I rested more and more often, and each time found it harder to get back on my feet. The grey light of dawn was showing in the eastern sky when I was forced to admit that I could go no further. I was on a sort of cart track which was a crazy-patterned river of slime. My head swam and I was as often on my knees as on my feet. Ahead loomed the ghostly shapes of a cluster of buildings, a farm. I was all in. I was beaten. I must have water, attention, rest. Without willing myself I staggered and slithered towards the buildings. The track became a stone path that led to the door of a house. I supported myself against the lintel and beat weakly on the panel with my fist. There was a long silence during which I swayed and struggled to remain conscious. Then, with a low scuffling sound and the rattle of a chain, the door was opened a mere six inches.

"Water, please", I babbled. "Air Force – Anglais – Ecosse."

I was suddenly inside the house and in pitch blackness. The door clicked behind me and the chain rattled. A match scraped and I screwed my eyes against the light as a candle was lit. A dark, lean, almost emaciated face, suspended above the flame, gazed intently at me out of black pools of eyes. The look was tangible as touch. For perhaps a minute I stood motionless, submissive, while the eyes took in every detail of my appearance. There was no sound, no word. Then the eyes shifted, a hand moved, and I followed the candle and the shadowy figure along the passage seeking support from the wall as I went. We passed through a door, crossed a cobbled yard and entered a small barn. The man, tall and spare I could now see, in shirt sleeves and with a tasselled woollen cap on his head, led me to a far corner, shifted some straw, and pulled a trap in the floor. He began to descend a rough wooden ladder, held the candle high and signed me to follow. It was as much as I could do to hold on to the rungs as I climbed down. At the bottom he stood still with the candle held aloft. There were six blanket-covered figures lying on the floor. One of these rose and came over.

"Hi Johnny. You've been a long time getting here." The Skipper's voice still held his quiet smile. My own voice was thick and drunken and I had difficulty with the words.

"Twenty-nine and a half trips make a tour, Skip?" I think he caught me as I fell.

# Death of an Android

Design One placed her fingers on the processing pad and thought-locked into the VDU.

*Memorandum*

> **To**: First Lord, Datalab (Planet 3) in high orbit.
> **From**: Design One, Android Design Division.
> **Ref**: 7th generation hybrids, end of series.

My Lord,

> Recent demat recovery, following complete operational break-down, of the final unit of the above series whose last report, emanating from position Midsea Coastal Region E3, is appended, marks the end of 3 millennia (local temporal computation) and 7 generations of experimental hybrids.

Design One frowned momentarily at what "Enhancement" did to the literary style of her plain thoughts. Despite the heroic achievements of this machine in the fields of thought scattering and fragmentation in telepathic transmission, she never quite warmed to it. Just as there were idioms that did not translate from tongue to tongue, so there were thoughts that were better left non-verbal.

> We at Design are proud of the long history of development and improvement represented by this series...

She permitted herself a small vanity.

> ... and hold in especially high regard the 7th generation agents now finally withdrawn from service. We believe that, in these androids, we ultimately achieved the optimum mix of pre-programming (PP) and environmental learning space (ELS), and that their use of semi-automatic telemetry (SAT) and the emergency system of plain language telepathic transmission (PLTT) produced the major breakthrough in anthropological study techniques which has contributed so

much to the high reputation of this complex.

D. One smiled to herself. This was a larger vanity which was not
really ameliorated by her sharing it around. However...

> At all stages of the planning, design and
> development of this vast enterprise, the
> highest priority has been given to the
> Galactic Rules for Observers (GRO), and
> this has never been more true, or more
> perfectly exemplified, than in the 7th
> generation studies now complete. At no
> time has the effect of the observer upon
> the observed been other than absolutely
> minimal. On no occasion have indige-
> nous cultures been altered in the slight-
> est by the presence, the actions, or the
> attitudes of our agents. The histories of
> peoples move on untroubled by our
> proximity.

She winced slightly at the rising pomposity and wondered, not
for the first time, if high brass really thrived on pap and platitude.

> Now of course, with the activating of our
> 8th generation units in whom telemetry
> has been made, not only fully automatic,
> but also subliminal, and PP has been lim-
> ited to the unconscious, leaving the
> entire conscious space open to environ-
> mental learning, we are less constrained
> by GRO. Since the observer will be a
> product, to all intents and purposes, of
> the culture he is observing, his effect
> upon it will be neither greater nor less
> than that of any indigenous individual.
> We are most confident the success of this
> approach will be the subject of future
> reports.

Your servant, my Lord,
Design One.

There follows:

> Enhanced fragmentary report in PLTT to
> Lords of Datalab (Planet 3) in high orbit,
> from Agent 7/333 in the field.

My telemetry has already failed due to severe buffeting and spik-
ing and the massive loss of fluid from an open wound. These con-
ditions are beyond the normal range of my self-healing
programmes, and besides, I have been deprived of most of my

mobility.

Dematerialised recovery would be possible at this stage, but in the interests of project security, I advise against it. There is a habit of post-death entombment here, and I have one or two associates courageous enough to remain close by who have this service in mind for me. Such interment should afford you the opportunity for clandestine dematerialisation and no one need ever know.

The end of this agent's transmission is imminent. These transmissions are dependent upon the last dregs of my low-power back-up systems. I will remain on stream until it is no longer possible but you must allow for progressive degradation of the purity of process.

Of course the strictly scientific data which have been the product of all these years of telemetry are finished. Your storage banks must bulge with them. What remains, by the very nature of this communication, belongs to the psyche I have had to develop to make it appear I am one of these people.

These people! These people are barbarous, for all their theocratic arrogance. Perhaps the one is a symptom of the other. They have a long history of enslavement and even now are ruled by occupation forces they obey as a matter of military realism and feel superior to as a matter of dogmatic certainty. The tribal chiefs and priests show more interest in what they call "The Law", meaning theology and politics, than in the fates of the ordinary men and women of their own society.

Indeed it was some injudicious utterances on my part regarding the importance of the plain man, which I based on the eclectic philosophies learned during my time with the desert monks, compounded by some simple hi-tech conjuring I felt obliged to use to cover up the more glaring inconsistencies in my assumed persona, and a few examples of contact healing I could not resist, that, finally, brought me to my present pass.

I do not always see clearly the crowd in front of me. Faces seem to advance and recede like the waves on the shore. The crowd is thinner, I think, than it was. Perhaps some have grown tired of enjoying another's pain and gone home to their own. Sometimes I see, or imagine I see, a small group of familiar, friendly faces, guardedly anxious.

Two women, their heads covered, stand a little away from the throng. They stand unhappily, waiting. I know them. The younger one is she who thought to educate me in the practices and rituals of love-making and the variations on the act of love. She was an assiduous teacher who insisted on frequent revision.

The other, the older one is used to sadness. Long ago she lost her only son to the paranoid decree of some demented despot. Recently she seems to have adopted me, and I think has come to regard me as flesh of her flesh and blood of her blood, which is the flowery terminology in common usage. Now she is about to lose me, and her sadness is crowned with sadness.

Both women watch anxiously, weep silently, suffer separately and together.

This, my Lords, is a world of sacrifice. Animals and produce and sometimes people are sacrificed to propitiate unheeding gods. The tears of women are sacrificed upon the altar of deceit, men's principles to greed, and freedom to expediency. Love is sacrificed to lust, and fair bodies are spiked upon trees as diversion for the multitude. This, my Lords...

Lords! Lords, I weaken. What am I then? Am I a man? Am I a machine in the body of a man? God in the machine? Am I then a sacrifice? A woman weeps. A woman weeps for me.

Lords! Why am I forsaken?

# User Friendly

FEATS 4 JD.
TO FEATS 1 LY.
8 FEB 1988.

OK, OK, Boss! Why you send me? No compren Swahili.
  Drinkipoos, post shift?
                              Joe.


FEATS 1 LY.
TO FEATS 4 JD.
8 FEB 1988.

At a loss to understand. You have VDU sickness? New Tech
Melancholia?
  Bevy def.
                              Lachlan.


FEATS 4 JD.
TO FEATS 1 LY.
8 FEB 1988.

Who sent gobbledegook story to FEATSFILE 4 under title,
"Blooter Blat", byline Jax McLown, nonsense dateline?
  Refreshment imperative.
                              Joe.

FEATS 1 LY.
TO FEATS 4 JD.
8 FEB 1988.

No Features desk admits to knowledge of any such story. Flash
me contents of FEATSFILE 4, but tomorrow.
 See you Cirrhosis Bar,
  Lachlan.


FEATS 1 LY.
TO ED 1 PQ.
9 FEB 1988.

Reporting strange story under unknown byline and title, of
impossible date, found in FEATSFILE 4.
 Not raised by any Features desk.
 Systems say story under such ident cannot possibly gain
access to computer.
 Presence in FEATSFILE 4 inexplicable.
 Comments please,
  Lachlan.


ED 1 PQ.
TO FEATS 1 LY.
9 FEB 1988.

Intriguing, dear boy.
 Flash me story. Bare all.
 Care for jar, apres ski?
  P.Q.

FEATS 1 LY.
TO ED 1 PQ.
10 FEB 1988.

Jar gratefully anticipated.
  Copy follows,

                                      Lachlan.


SCOTTIS NEWSPAP.
GLECK HERL.
SATFEB 2, 3990.
TITLE, BLOOTER BLAT.
BLINE, JAX McLOWN.

A wee cloudfu red snow clobbed us on its wy to Ebra. When I
say 'wee' I speak cosmic. It wir big enug to red-out Greater
Gleck fro Greenk to Lingston.

The mint we sot, we kint thae blud Centrals fro Lund wir
respons. Ersins The Blud Thatch, twa thous yr ago, ett Scot babs
and we devolved unilat, thae bast suthrons ha tried recolon us.

Thas wy we haddy mak Nobosland twix Hadris Wal and
Mankis Shipanal.

Red snow wir sumt new. We scrapt up and sent fr analys and
spect the wurz. The wurz we got.

Thwir no direc effec on Yins or Yans, but expos to
Redsnohaze wir catastrop to omnisex androids. Thir hormolin-
semino systems wir contam bi deneutralis enzyms, and aredy,
sev thous Yins wir impreg bi Lundi clones.

"Rape!" we craw to Eurogov, and Eurogov castigs Lundigov fr
the millioth time in twa thous yr fr its repress and arrogy wys.
Lundigov produc statists ti pruf thir the oldsa and the bes, and
aywy, Eurogov's Laws too muc justic fr Lundigov Oboy Network.

So whas new? We litral left holden babs. Ancien Scottis Mottis:
Semper in excretis, toujours la poliskoosh.

Scottisgov expelt fames Lundi novler, Danis Deflat, cot
emyfyvan in Trongat. A wek respon, satisfyin nun.

Diploscots, lobidossen in Europarl, won recrd compen at
Lund's expens to process futur clones thro Scottis edusyst. Al

Yins, Redsno-insem, wir giv freepard fr illegl pregs.

Figs fr emigrat fro Canda and Austral to Scottis wir adjust to balans incres in indig pop, and Sonkildy wir reopen.

Al omnisex androids wir scrap and Eurojig replac wi lates mods, no charg.

Bi twa yr, al lanmines in Nobosland wir replac bi Tartan Snow mods and Lund wir informt.

STAT QUO STAB.

ED 1 PQ.
TO FEATS 1 LY.
11 FEB 1988.

Official explanation: Systems hiccup.

Personal View: Another 'blud' computer going all creative.

Action advised (*ex cathedra*): Scrub out FEATSFILE 4. Forget entire episode.

STAT QUO STAB.

You owe me jar, dear boy,

P.Q.

FETS 4 JAX.
TO FETS 1 XAV.
MONFEB 4, 3990.

Wharell mi stry, date SATFEB 2?

Fylt FETSFYL 4. Gon blud limbo.

Kerfr snif?

Jaxie.

PS. Wha funct red butt, mrk TIMEPOST?

# Eck Spots the Mark

I particularly noticed that the air appeared to be the same thickness when Eck vanished into it. Another cherished cliché down the tube. There was a slight chill, but nobody ever vanishes into cold air, or warm air, or any air other than thin.

We had been enjoying a face-to-face conversation in George Square at Sir Walter Scott's bottom. I sat on a Corporation bench trying misanthropically to look like a full complement. He sat facing me, three or four feet off the ground, on a kind of magic carpet of cloud. He was a spindly wee man in a gold lamé nappy, but he seemed relaxed enough in a multi-jointed, multi-pointed Lotus position.

"Whit's your name?" says I.

"You can call me Alexis", he says, and his voice was a nasal Tannoy, as though he had learned his English on the Airdrie to Helensburgh line at Low Level, Queen Street.

"Alexis? That's a bit Merchant City. D'ye mind if ah shorten it tae Eck?"

"Please yourself. It's a nom de whatsitsname anyway. I'm surprised though, that you're not surprised to see me."

"Och! There's no much surprises me nowadays. Ah'm 68 years of age, an ah fought the Second World War, sometimes single-handed. Efter Hitler, Stalin, Thatcher an the Ayatollah thur's damn few surprises left. Besides, ah know whut you are."

He gave me a look. "That's interesting. Whut am I then?"

"You," I savoured, "are a dissociated dysfunction. You are an externalised hallucination. You are a pint of heavy gone mental."

He smiled, half-saluted, and performed the thin air trick previously mentioned.

For a while I sat looking at the fluted stalk of rock surmounted by Sir Wattie and wondered if the word 'ABBOTSFORD' went all the way through.

"An by the way," I said skywards, "ah was never able tae finish *Ivanhoe*." Then I went home.

Home was a highrise in Sighthill. I keep it clean right enough in memory of Bella. Well, reasonably clean, but I admit it was, as usual, a bit throuither. There was a long envelope on the mat just inside the outside door. I am not fond of long envelopes. They tend to be carriers, either of advertisers' lies, or creditors' truths, both equally unwelcome. This one was not ordinary. It had my name on it, beautifully printed in italic script, but no address, and no stamp. Hand-delivered? I opened it and took out the postcard-size coloured snap it contained. Some photo! The background had caught one lion and one corner of the Cenotaph, and beyond, a good lump of the façade of the Municipal Buildings. Foreground left: there was yours aye lounging nonchalantly on my exclusive municipal bench, a cynical eyebrow raised, a sceptical ear cocked, and, foreground right: there, with knobbly elbows gesticulating, knobbly knees Lotussed, golden hippin screaming modesty, perched on dry ice in mid air, Little Alexis, Wee Eck. On the back of the card, a one-word question in that perfect italic script:

*Hallucination?*

I took the remains of a tin of beans out of the fridge, toasted some bread, made the tea and switched on the telly in time for the news: official inquiries into oil-rig disasters, airline disasters, rail disasters. Politicians talking fast to prevent interruption, using words to mask meaning. Lying bastards! Yorkshire soap about cows and a pub. Lancashire soap about drinking and a pub. London soap about the Police Force and several pubs, designed to undermine confidence in Laura Norder. Scottish Questions. English answers. Dozing off. Dozing off. Dozed off.

I woke to the all-through-the-night rubbish and doused the picture. My mouth was like a crematorium, so I put the kettle on and asked Eck if he would like some tea. He shook his head and sat patiently on his cushion halfway up the living-room wall, his back to Bella's favourite print of the wee boy and the teardrop. I took to rattling crockery in the kitchen. I can be rotten when I like and I deliberately worked to rule on the tea-making. At last however, I sat down on the old settee and confronted him from behind my steaming mug.

"Okay," I Spencer-Tracied, "let's have it."

He took his time, gave me the searching-look routine, furrowed brow and all. He was no slouch himself when it came to the rule book.

"Do you know," he asked finally, "what a sleeper is?"

"Ah jist woke up."

"No, I mean in the John Le Carré sense."

"Oh aye. Is he a railwayman?"

"He writes spy stories."

"Ah! That kinda sleeper."

"That kind of sleeper." His searching look, I realised, was actually a shrewd look. He knew fine I was pulling his proverbial. "Actually," he twinkled, "you are one of us."

"Away! Ah've never wore gold lamé in ma life."

"Not that you remember."

"Right! Not that ah remember."

"Oh, the memories will rush back, once I have performed some psychic unblocking on you, once I have pulled a few triggers."

I was not at all chuffed about blocked triggers. "Ah'm no too happy aboot surgery", I told him.

"Surgery does not play any part. Nothing physical is involved. It is purely a mental process, and it can be performed remotely. In fact, there was no need for me to be here in the first place. I came along for old time's sake."

"We've met before?"

"We are very closely related, but your memory of that was blocked when you were reconceived."

"Reconceived?"

He smiled his funny wee twinkly smile. "Don't be worried by words. As one of the poets of your city says, 'Words are instruments that torture images.' Don't be worried about anything."

"Ah'm no worried." And neither I was. Ever since Bella died I seemed to be just going through the motions, waiting for something to happen. At last something was happening. "Ah'm no worried."

"Good!" he smiled. "I suggest you take pen and paper and write down, in your own voice, all that has occurred since we met yesterday in George Square. This will divert your mind into the state best suited to the next part of the process. It may interest you to know that what you write will be transcribed, made presentable, and will land on the desk of a friendly editor."

He took to the thin air again and left me gazing into the tear-stained face of Bella's wee boy. I rose, collected pad and ballpoint from the drawer in Bella's sideboard, sat down at the table and wrote:

"I particularly noticed that the air appeared to be the same thickness when Eck vanished into it..."

# White, With One Sugar

There are two things that send the aficionados of detective fiction up the wall: the jigsaw metaphor, and the use of coincidence. They have the same effect on real policemen, which was why, after I telephoned and made an appointment to see Doctor Margaret Rintoul the following evening, I took out my notes and had a last look at the jigsaw of transparent coincidences which fitted together so beautifully but made no picture. I gathered my thoughts.

I had never heard of chemical castration until I came across the phrase casually used in one of those ultra-feminist articles on rape that occasionally appear in the Glossies. Later that same morning Sam Craig, our pathologist, sat next to me during a briefing, and afterwards, in conversation, I confessed my ignorance and asked him to explain.

"Chemical castration?" he repeated. "Funny you should ask."

"Why funny?"

"Well, not funny. A coincidence really. Talking to a mate of mine only yesterday, an endocrinologist, and he was telling me that, for the first time in his career, he had, not one, but two patients, two young blokes, referred to him last week displaying all the symptoms of chemical castration: loss of libido, impotence, testosterone levels haywire, the lot. Even faint signs of subcutaneous bruising on the abdomen where a needle might have been used. No connection between the two. Referred by different GPs from different districts on different dates. Both denied any knowledge of how they came to be injected and neither showed any signs of being takers of any of the usual muck."

It sounded mysterious, but was a bit too vague and too medical for my interest. On the faint possibility of an illegal drugs connection I asked Craig if he could discreetly get me the names and addresses. He pretended shock.

"Not at all ethical, but I'll see what I can do."

Two days later they were on my desk and I mentally promised an obsequy on the compassionate pathologist when the time came. Meanwhile I passed the names on to the computer and asked it to earn its keep. One was clean, nothing known. The other had no convictions, but rated a short story. He was the subject of a complaint by a woman who accused him of a series of obscene phone calls, claiming she had recognised his voice in spite of his attempts to disguise it. He was questioned at length but there was insufficient evidence to justify action. The file ended euphemistically. A 'friendly warning' was issued and he was released. I had a quiet smile to myself. I've issued the odd friendly warning in my time.

It was a routine, almost reflex action on my part to request the computer's thoughts on Obscene Telephone Calls reported in this area over, say, the last two years. It was not a very long list. Most OTCs are casual, one-off affairs made to accompany masturbation, with numbers taken at random and rung one-by-one until a female voice replies. The only cases likely to involve police action are the persistent ones where calls are made frequently and at all times of the day and night. Apart from the sexual connotations these are apparently designed to frighten. Even these are fraught with difficulties for the police and it is seldom that anyone is ever caught.

My eye picked up Sam Craig's name on the readout, and I concentrated on the particular entry. It concerned the death of one Jennifer Somerville, aged 30, spinster, barbiturate overdose, self-administered. Post-mortem: Sam Craig. The body was discovered by Margaret Rintoul and Susan Bissett, friends of the deceased, who gave evidence of a history of depression and an acute reaction to recent experience of obscene and frightening phone calls.

I phoned Sam Craig and was lucky to get him in.

"What do you remember about the death of Jennifer Somerville? OD."

"Remind me of the details.."

I did, but he interrupted halfway through my summary.

"I've got it now," he said, "It was the first I'd seen of Maggie Rintoul since we were at Med School."

"You knew her? And she's a doctor?"

"Yeah. She's a GP now, and I did know her. Beautiful she was. Pity about the three Ps."

"Three Ps?"

"Proclivities Precluding Pricks." Pathologists, apparently, are no more delicate than policemen. "Still at it", he continued. "Shares a flat with a good-looking chick called Suzie Something who's a computer brain with Telecom or somebody. Mind you, they were pretty upset about the suicide. Seemed to be very fond of the girl. Well, they would be, wouldn't they? What did you want to know?"

"Oh, that'll do for now", I said, thanked him, and rang off. I had things to think about, and while I was doing that I wandered downstairs to have a word with Reilly, our tame electronics man. "What's the state-of-the-art in the call-tracing business?" I wanted to know. Reilly was enthusiastic and spoke for about fifteen minutes without taking pause. Evidently the new electronic exchanges, now fully operational in most of the urban areas, have opened the way to all sorts of marvels. Tracing calls is now a piece of cake. He'd even seen a prototype box which, when attached to a handset, flashed up the phone numbers of callers. Feed a number into the right computer and in seconds you have a name, an address, and maybe even what the caller had for breakfast.

So I phoned Dr. Margaret Rintoul, made an appointment for the next evening, scrutinised my notes, decided I had no criminal without a crime, no murderer without a murder, no case. What I had was an itch, and a need to scratch.

The door was opened by a dark-haired, strikingly handsome woman in her mid-thirties. I flashed my warrant card. "Detective Inspector Strachan. I have an appointment with Doctor Rintoul."

"I'm Maggie Rintoul. Come in." She smiled me through the hall into a sitting room which, though trendily artistic, suggested underlying comfort. She indicated the younger woman seated at the coffee table fiddling with cups and cakes and things. "My flatmate, Susan Bissett. You wanted a word with both of us, I think you said."

I nodded, accepted a seat and coffee (white, with one sugar), and allowed my antennae free rein during the formalities. They were good, these two. There was no discernible strain. They put me at my ease and, by God, they were a couple of smashers. I dismissed the faint twinge of regret as a sexist emotion unworthy of my normal, even-handed approach. After all, what they did in private was their own business and, in any event, my view of it was based on pretty sketchy evidence. Besides, it was hardly germane to the case. The Case! That was a laugh.

"Well, Inspector, what can we do for you?" Maggie Rintoul's voice scattered all my ifs and buts, my besides and after-alls.

"To Hell with it!" I thought. "Cards on the table time." I took a deep breath. "I would like to speak to you, ladies," I said, "about the suicide of Jennifer Somerville and about obscene phone calls. I would like to give you my views on revenge by proxy, and vigilantes, and seek your views on chemical castration using Goserilin under some form of general anaesthetic, and I would like to speak about hi-tech telephone number tracing, and perhaps I could have another coffee, white please, with one sugar."

# Two Diaries From Eleanor

*Another year. Another diary from Eleanor. Rain this morning. Cleared in the afternoon. Bitterly cold.*

What the hell am I going to do with a diary?

"Be creative", Eleanor said. She bought two. "I always give Daddy a diary for New Year." The other was for me. "Be creative", she commanded. That's El all over – commanding. Her old man never struck me as the Dear Diary type.

"He's not. It's become almost a tradition with him, a way of hanging on to his little girl. I give him one every year and he feels obliged to put something in it. I've been through them: next to nothing but daily weather reports."

That's El all over, a peeper into other people's diaries. "Be creative", she tells me, which is what I have been trying to do, spreading over several diary days in the doing, and then she begins removing my clothes, which makes writing creatively quite difficult. And then she stands before me and begins removing her own clothes, which renders any further literature, for the time being, out of the ques…

…tion. That's El all over. "Be creative", she says, then goes all procreative. That was last night. Tonight she is the model student, glasses on, working through the books, writing an essay on Social Science. Of course, if it goes well, if the essay pleases her, I am likely to suffer further assault. I am astonished sometimes, how tenuous is the hold that creativity exerts upon the artist, how easily he is persuaded to abandon his most cherished ideals, how equivocal his artistic integrity.

That frown of concentration and the ballpoint tapping on her

105

bottom lip make her look like a child. The hair falling over her forehead betrays the adolescent. The T-shirt and the Levi's proclaim the woman.

I will entitle my masterpiece, *The Fall*. It will be a tragedy for unaccompanied voice, and the hero will be a poet, Sebastian.

*No call from Eleanor this week. I expect she is busy with her studies. Dull and misty morning. Watery sunshine in the afternoon. Still cold. Wind rising.*

## The Fall

The brown leaf, superfluous now, fell crazy-paved on the kinetic air. Sebastian watched its feverish descent into the abyss of his mind. "My life," he thought, "a fin-flutter in the deep, a transient, phosphorescent gleam in the blackness." A poem almost brinked his imagination, trembled for birth, and was lost. Only a line remained, part of a line:

"Brown leaf on the timeless ether..."

The leaf swirled. A little insect man straddled its back. Glorious, this riding of the air-surf, exciting, this bending of the body to the pull of invisible currents: side-slide-glide-slip-flip-skip. But the strongest pull is downwards, little insect man without wings, always downwards.

*Eleanor brought some of her friends home tonight. Seem a very decent bunch of youngsters. They had some beer with them but decided they liked my Bordeaux and my Soave better. One was particularly keen on my single malt. The rest called him Sebastian although apparently his name is Tom. Most of their conversation was beyond me. Sebastian/Tom has long hair. Eleanor appears quite taken with him. The weather today has been neither one thing nor the other. There is a threat of rain later.*

"Gravity", Sebastian cried. "Damn Gravity! Damn the force that drags a man's spiritual guts to Hell's centre, and damn the women who hook his belt and speed his fall."

Phoebe hooked. Phoebe had freckles on her breast.

> Oh her breast is freckled,
> Speckled to the nipple,
> And the ripple of her skin
> Is sin.

Sin is the acceptance of gravity. Sin is the passionate desire to link arms and fall. Sin atrophies the wings.

Slish... his foot on wet grass. Phoebe's bottom would get wet if they sat down. It would become pulpy like his brain, or like a baked bean by Dali, a baked bean or, what was that picture – *An Atmospherocephalic Bureaucrat Milking A Cranial Harp?*

> *Eleanor rang twice this week. Unusual. Hope she is all right. Says she is, but twice in one week makes me uneasy. Quite nice out today, almost like Spring.*

Phoebe was an Autumn creature, tawny-haired. He was the leaf she rode. Why did she have to love him in her no-demanding way? Why did her silence command him? Why did he make demands upon himself for her, this tawny-haired, tawny-eyed, tawny-brained, autumnal creature? She hyphenated his mind. He was a sugar-sweet, syrup-tasted, saccharin-flavoured phrase-maker. His words should be active and scintillating like sparks of flint.

"I am a poet." Sebastian addressed the tree. "Seduced from my legitimate despair by a speckled breast and a loin, sheathed but naked. I am dead, entombed within respectable debauchery, phallus-in-amber stood on Phoebe's shelf."

*Eleanor spent the entire weekend with us. Not often we see her by herself. Not much to say. I feel she is not happy. Wish she would trust me, let me help. Weather back to gloom. Cloudy. Showery.*

The tree was more masculine, more controlled, not tempted to lust out of season. Sad oboes played in trees at autumn time. There was something about a tree against a darkening sky, something...

> I love the tree in a minor key,
> Sombre and wood-
> wind-tousled, Arpeggios controlled
> By the baton, Wind,
> Brooding as night falls
> On the sad symphony
> That God composes
> And Nature conducts.
>
> I love its black notes
> As the sap stills
> In falling cadences,
> And Hope, that agonised us
> In the day,
> Fades, with the tree,
> In a dark diminuendo,
> And leaves us peace.

But there was little peace, and hope was the Devil's most potent instrument. Hope it was that saved us from suicide, preserved us for misery. Phoebe was full of hope. He could visualise her now, walking across the park, her heels going click-clack, click-clack on the paving. She would appear far off and he would stand and watch her thighs shaping the tight skirt and her breasts bobbing with every step.

"I hope you haven't been waiting long." She hoped, she hoped.

God dammit! Couldn't she see he'd spent his whole future waiting? But always, when he saw her, and when she smiled with her mouth and with her eyes, he felt the gravitational pull of her body, and abandoned himself to chaos. Always he trembled.

*No word from Eleanor for more than a week. Weather
thin and sour.*


"Tyranny!" Sebastian said to the tree. The tree shrugged a shower
of leaves and sighed as it watched them fall. "I won't stand it,"
Sebastian cried again, '"this murderous rule of fear. I will not be
cowed like the rest of the mob, the ones you see on buses, in
the streets, leaving offices. You've only to look at them, look at
their faces, look at their eyes.

> Watch their eyes,
> Stand on the pavement, watch
> Their tired eyes,
> Hotch-potch
> Of humanity,
> Sick souls
> In a sick city
> Seeking holes.
> Maybe the children see clear,
> But even they know fear.

He was a jelly no longer. He had sacrificed his art and his life
to mere futility. No more! Now was the time to break, to make
an end, maybe a beginning too, a time to open his wings and
soar out and beyond gravity. No looking down, no last fond
farewells, no tender embraces. He must purge himself finally,
brutally.

His eyes espied her now across the park. She moved quickly
towards him. He watched her thighs shape her skirt, and felt her
bobbing breasts at every step. He heard the click-clack, click-
clack of her heels on the paving.

A lone, brown leaf, falling from the tree, side-slipped on the
bodies of its dead brothers, and became anonymous.


*It has rained constantly all of this miserable day.*

# The Man Who Wasn't Anything

Barney McColl was a dab hand at squaring up a character. Prided himself on it. "Gie me five minutes' crack in a pub wi a punter," he would say, "nah'll hiv um taped. Ah'll tell ye 'is religion, 'is politics, whut team he supports, 'is wife's name, how minny weans they've goat, whut he diz furra livin, the lot."

This was approximately true, and it was not merely nosiness on his part. People did tell him things, often very personal things, and – just as often – with an air of gratitude for his having listened. Barney appeared genuinely interested in people, and most people responded.

There were limits, though, to Barney's insight. Had he been more sophisticated he might have been a successful blackmailer or even a novelist. As it was, he suffered a deep-seated insecurity in his relations with others that was only assuaged by his ability to label their *curricula vitae* and slot them into the filing cabinet that was his mind.

He had his little failures of course, but as long as he gleaned enough significant information to take the bare look off the pigeonhole, he wasn't unduly perturbed. Not, that is, until Lanky began using The Cirrhosis Bar for a slow, reflective half of lager five or six evenings every week. "Lanky" was the descriptive name Barney, in his own mind, bestowed on this tall, thin, solemn man in the dark, nondescript raincoat and the brown corduroy bunnet. So quietly self-effacing was he, and so short were his evening visits, that nearly two weeks went by before Barney noticed their regularity and considered it necessary to label him with even an interim *nom de convenience*. So it was an unspoken "Lanky", for the time being, and a friendly nod from Barney whenever he caught the other's eye, which, it had to be conceded, was seldom. Barney found himself thinking that this was the least roving eye he had ever tried to catch. It seemed to be fixed on an unspecified point beyond the pub gantry with a sort of unfocused look that somehow suited, and even contributed to, the solemnity of the long, narrow face and its tracery of fine lines, and its grey-stippled designer stubble.

It was not long before Barney came to feel thoroughly frustrated by attempts at eye contact which foundered at the bridge of Lanky's nose. He pushed his luck, and landed himself in one of the most unproductive conversations he had ever experienced. He ordered himself a pint of heavy, carried it across to the small round table near the door where Lanky absently caressed the remains of his lager, and sat down.

"Quiet the night."

"Aye."

"You live near?"

"Naw."

"You work near?"

"Naw."

"What brings ye intae this pub?"

"Jist passin."

Lanky drained his glass, rose, gave a short nod to a Barney apparently suspended in the middle distance, and left. Barney was astounded. Here was a guy with no name, no job, no home, no regular pub, no dress sense, no expression on his face, a guy who wasn't anything, but a guy who could leave you feeling as though you were invisible. Barney quickly ordered another pint of heavy and worried his way round it.

A couple of weeks later his worry had become an obsession. Sarah Hosie's Bar, affectionately known as The Cirrhosis Bar, because, Barney claimed, Sarah was a loose liver, had been his favourite howff for years. Now, more and more, it became merely a place where he drank morosely and concocted schemes for breaking down Lanky's reserve. He tried everything. He offered drinks which were always refused. Lanky stuck to his one half of lager and never stretched it to last more than thirty minutes. Barney broached every subject under the sun to raise a spark of interest: football, snooker, horses, religion, politics, money, booze, women. Nothing worked. Lanky failed to react. He body-swerved, or displayed indifference in monosyllables. Barney almost became convinced that his half-joke about Lanky not being anything had more than a hint of truth to it. He was a hollow man, empty, a shell, a nonentity, a ghost. But Barney knew this was a cop-out. If you labelled somebody as nothing, then your label was nothing, and your filing cabinet contained nothing, and you were faced with an enigma, and enigmas were a serious source of insecurity.

Barney brooded, and drank more than was good for him, and brooded some more. It was ridiculous that he should be so affected by his failure to place this person in a manageable setting. He was scenting mysteries where none existed. He was dealing with a man, an ordinary human being, not some wraith that dematerialised into the night air when he left the pub, not some Count Dracula who changed into a bat the moment he stepped to the west of Partick Cross. He was making mountains out of smoke rings, and it was high time he did something concrete about it. Lanky had to go somewhere when he crossed the pub threshold and went outside. There had to be someplace ordinary where he lived an ordinary life as an ordinary guy. There had to be someplace where he was anchored to reality. He had to be followed, and Barney had to be the man to follow him.

When the time came, it was on a night when Lanky arrived at the bar a little later than usual, and left a little later than usual, and Barney had drunk a little more than usual, and nearly missed his cue. He was a couple of minutes behind Lanky when he stepped out into the cold night. He suffered a momentary disorientation as the beer fumes in his head reacted to the toxic freshness of the air. The speed with which he retrieved his equilibrium owed more to years of practice than his physical fitness. There was no sign of Lanky, but Barney was not fazed. Reconnaissance patrols had previously sketched Lanky's immediate route on leaving the pub. He always turned left, then left again into the lane, passed the pub car park, and onwards to the west. The way was quite well lit. There were two high-power lamps in the car park and streetlights along the lane at regular intervals.

Barney made his second left and adjusted his focus, expecting to see Lanky in the distance. Instead, he became aware of group activity about fifty yards or so up the lane including thuds and curses and fists and feet flying. A kicking was in progress. Sober, Barney would have considered discretion. Now, before he could think, he bawled at the top of his considerable voice, "Whut the bliddy hell's gaun oan here?" The result was magic. Half a dozen figures suddenly lost interest in what they were doing and took off westwards like the wind. They left what looked like a bundle of rags lying on the ground under one of the street lights. Barney came close. It was Lanky. He lay flat on his back, his arms outstretched on either side. The corduroy bunnet was gone, and his grey hair stuck out spikily all round his head. There was blood on his face and a pool of it spreading it from under his coat. He was very still.

"Oh Jesus Christ!" Barney said. "Jesus Christ!" A bizarre thought came into his head and was immediately dismissed. It was the drink. Time to be practical, time to go back to the pub and get somebody to ring the police. He turned away, then turned back and took a last, long look at Lanky. "Anywey," he said. "Ah know whut ye ur noo. Yur a bliddy corpse."

# Winter Solstice

With its customary precision, even in the darkness of a December night, the Auto-Gondola negotiated the complexities of the atmosphere lock on the Glasgow Dome, swished along the final stages of the co-ordinal track to the Green, and settled, as though weightless, in front of the People's Palace. Noble Kell disembarked and, since his journey was one-way, pressed the return button on the Gondola. He watched its soft glow disappear into the night as it headed for the Dome outlet and computed its course to Regional Distribution, probably somewhere in Scandinavia.

Burning his boats! That was not the sad thought it might at first appear; just tidying his desk, just one of the habits of efficiency. He turned towards the single light in the main entrance to the People's Palace. It must be nearly three centuries since he was last here, about the time they began building the Dome and declared Glasgow a Museum of Culture. The Palace itself had always been a museum of course, one he had loved all through his childhood, and he had his own reasons for visiting it now.

He had his reasons also for choosing the date, the winter solstice, not reasons that would impress, or make much sense to his colleagues, idiosyncratic reasons, a hobbyhorse, perhaps, and giving a more than casual nod towards a symbology that had enslaved most of the human race for several millennia. He had been introduced to the study of Comparative Mythology in his youth. It had opened his eyes and his mind and, in due course, had led him along paths that had opened his spirit. But all that is by the way. Earning the Prize of the Nobles had earned him the right to choose, and he had chosen this time and this place.

As he entered the museum it lit up automatically. Perhaps by association, an old poem came into his mind complete. It was a *fin de siècle* piece from the pen of some long-forgotten, fifth-rate, Glasgow poet of the fag end of the twentieth century, a period which fascinated him, a time when every district seemed to boast a Council-funded writer's workshop which encouraged ill-educated labourers and shop girls to turn out demotic free verse by the ream. This anonymous piece had stuck in his memory because it summed up for him the decadence that preceded the demise of all those great world religions whose origins lay so plainly in ancient solar astronomy, in Sun worship.

> The old Gods rode along the line
> of the ecliptic till it turned
> at Capricorn and made its first,
> fine, rising foray into winter.
>
> And this is where the old Gods chose
> their birth.
>
> The new Gods are no different.
> The Multis plan their boom around
> the solstice.
>
> Christ is reborn
> into a shopping mall.
>
> Atheists erect
> their Christmas trees.

He stood for a minute or two in the foyer coaxing his memory through the centuries. Yes, it was the same; the kiosk which dispensed picture-cards, booklets, old maps, all the paraphernalia of folk history and sheer nostalgia; the staircase that led to the upper floors; the doorway that took you through to the Winter Gardens.

He remembered that the exhibit he sought was on the first floor, so he mounted the staircase and, within minutes, found the rectangular opening representing a window through which he could look into the kitchen of a slum tenement in Glasgow, c. 1920.

He was unprepared for the emotional upsurge stirred within him by the reproduction of this tiny apartment and he stood, quite shaken, re-experiencing the long-forgotten taste of tears, striving to clarify the memories of a secure and sustaining breast, and the rush to the safety of a pair of muscular arms and the smell of sweat and pipe tobacco and sawdust.

The kitchen, he knew, was a fraud, a simulacrum, a museum piece, but it was as close to the reality as any memory of his could ever be, so close indeed, that he was prepared, for his own purposes, to accept it as real. That hole-in-the-wall bed was where he had been born. He was one of a small and diminishing number who had been conceived, carried to term, and delivered in the ancient manner. The space below the bed was hidden from view by a white piece of curtain material which his mother had originally called the pawn, but subsequently anglicised to valance. Behind this was stored the zinc bathtub used as a depository for soiled clothing awaiting washday, except on Friday nights, when it was dragged out on the linoleum in front of the fireplace for a marathon family scrubbing. The remaining space below the bed belonged to the kist, a beautifully dovetailed, cedar-lined box made by his father as an apprentice-piece, and lovingly used by his mother to hold her few spare blankets, sheets, and table covers.

Kell left his place at the window, walked round the side of the exhibit and entered the little kitchen through a small, dark lobby and a softwood door, scumbled and grained to look like oak. There were two wooden-armed chairs, one on each side of the iron grate, and he sat down, his back to the window. The ribbon on his left cuff displayed 0100 hours, which was about the time he had specified. He closed his eyes.

The Sun, in its annual journey, had already reached that point where the ecliptic touches the Tropic of Capricorn, where it appears to pause before it turns north and is reborn, only to flee the pursuit of the despot Winter. It is a time of darkness and seeming death, but also a time of growth and promise. The ecliptic rises degree by degree through the wintry months to the baptism of Spring, after which the waters of the earth are transformed into the wine of the vine, and the corn is harvested to make the loaves that will feed the multitude.

He felt a slight prickling sensation on the backs of his hands. He shivered and opened his eyes. His father sat in the chair opposite his own. It was his father as a young man, home from work, shirt-sleeved, smoking his pipe, reading his newspaper.

Kell sat perfectly still. This was actual, this he remembered, this had been real. From behind him he heard the chink of dishes at the sink and the sound of his mother's voice singing:

> He stood in a beautiful mansion
> Surrounded by riches untold.
> He gazed on a beautiful picture
> That hung in a frame of gold.
> Twas the picture of a lady
> So beautiful, young and fair...

116

Her voice was sweet and young and its music smoothed out the scratch in her accent. The light in the room, which had been softened to simulate ancient gaslight, brightened. The wall behind the recessed bed became a screen. A great throng of people appeared, lines and lines of them receding into the distance, faces and figures and costumes, familiar and unfamiliar, remembered and recognised, half-remembered, half-forgotten, people he had known through all the long years. His parents now stood in the front line of the host, appearing of an age more like his later memories of them. His mother's simple song changed, became a choral work for many voices. This great throng sang and waved and beckoned him. And the music swelled and swelled. And the light grew brighter and brighter and brighter.

# The Twist in O Henry's Tail

The confrontation, when it finally and inevitably took place, was on the rugged summit of Cheekbi Jowl overlooking the great, sun-drenched plain of Sara Ha. He wore no more than a skimpy loin clout, but I would have recognised him in any disguise.

"So it is you", I remarked.

"A man is not only known by the ferniticles on his back", he replied.

"True", I said.

"Nor will a blind man thank you for a looking-glass", he rejoined.

The conversation was taking an unexpected turn. I fingered my chin thoughtfully. It was of the utmost importance that I regain the initiative.

"Ah", I chuckled.

"The owl is grave," he mused, "not on account of its wisdom, but on account of its gravity."

I was compelled to a grudging admiration for the strange sagacity of this outlandish figure. Our presence on this broken summit suddenly seemed portentous, fated, predestined. I pinched myself in case it was a dream. It was not. I waited. Just as I expected, he spoke again.

"The wasp is a busy creature," he reflected, "but it still has time for sandwiches."

"What?" I ejaculated.

"The wise man makes a fool of himself three times a day", he gibed.

"He does?" I queried.

"No, that's not quite true", he conceded.

"No, it is not", I breathed.

"No", he parried.

"Why?" I prompted.

"Because", he asserted.

"What?" I spluttered.

"Yes", he grunted.

"Oh", I muttered.

"Scotch mist will soak an Englishman to the skin", he quipped.

"Yes", I agreed.

"Is that all you have to say?" he enquired, fixing me with that penetrating blue-eyed stare.

"Well, it did strike me," I mumbled, "that the Scotch mist thing had racist undertones."

"Camels complain, but the caravan reaches the oasis", he chaffed.

"You mean?" I started.

"The firefly is just a beetle with a battery", he lampooned.

"Ah, now I understand", I disclosed.

"You get it?" he demanded.

"Yes I do", I nodded.

"Sure?" he rumbled.

"Yes", I purred.

"Where?" he thundered.

"Well", I faltered.

"What?" he exploded.

"A cracked bell can never sound well ", I gritted.

"Ting-a-ling-a-ling", he tintinnabulated.

"Ding-dong", I carilloned. "Ding-dong", I tocsinned. "Ding-dong", I angelussed. "Ding-dong", I campaniled.

He scowled at me.

I scowled at him.

"Scowl, scowl", we glowered.

It was stalemate.

One of us had to die.

# The Shortbread Men

It was no more natural in the early 1950s than it is now for a man to eat his best friend, but love takes some in a queer way. It took Amby by the soul and twisted him until he hated as hard as he loved, and in the end you might say it was the death of him.

Until Jean MacDonald unknowingly introduced her trim dark person into our lives, Amby, Dougie and I were inseparable. "The Wild Ones", they called us in Blaeburn, although there was no malice in the name. Indeed, there was no malice in us. Since childhood we had had a name for mischief, and I think our ploys were more a result of our reputation than the reverse.

Individually we were as serious and useful as any man in the town. Amby and Dougie were masters in their own fields. Amby was a baker. He owned a small Home Bakery in St Mary Street, did all the oven-work himself, and employed two girls to serve in the shop.

"My Father", he once told me, "slaved away most of his life at bread and rolls to make enough to buy this place. His ambition was to do the finest shortbread in the country. He died too soon." At twenty-five, Amby carried on the tradition. His shortbread was in great demand and its fame spread far beyond the town limits. He lived alone and self-sufficient in a single room above the shop, did all his own cooking and cleaning, and insatiably read musty old books on witchcraft and black magic.

Dougie was an engineer. Motor cars were his life. He was head mechanic in McVey's Garage and, if there was anything in a car at all, Dougie was the man to bring it out. He was the original extrovert with a constant cheery grin, an uncontrollable shock of vivid red hair and a frankness of speech that could at times be embarrassing. He contrasted sharply with the tall darkness of Amby who inclined to introspection except in the matter of shortbread.

We were, all three, bachelors, though Dougie had set fluttering many a young female heart, and a number of mothers with marriageable daughters marked Amby down as a good match. But Amby had his shortbread and his witches, Dougie his cars, and, at the time, I was content with my job on the *Courier*. Occasionally, when we felt the need for excitement, we would tour the pubs and dance-halls of Blaeburn and the black country beyond in Dougie's old Ford.

It was on one of those excursions that we first met Jean. When we arrived late at the Town Hall, feeling the better for a few drams, there was a quickstep on. Jean danced by in the clutches of Joe Devlin, a weedy youth with a crew-cut, drape suit and orange socks. She was dressed in jade green and looked cool and fresh. Her black hair was cut short and curled into the nape of her neck. She looked and danced like a woodland elf.

Dougie cut in. My eyes followed them round the floor. Already the old patter was turned on. I saw the flash of her teeth as she smiled. I allowed them one round and then intervened.

"Excuse me." My courtesy was impeccable.

Dougie glared. "My seconds will call in the morning."

But I was away. Jean had no weight, and an instinct for dancing. I performed my repertoire of intricate steps. She followed as though we had been partners for years.

"You're a new face", I remarked.

She nodded. "We've just moved to Blaeburn." Her voice was black velvet, surprisingly deep for one so small and neat.

"From Edinburgh?"

"From Glasgow."

"But your accent..."

"I took elocution lessons." She laughed and I launched her into my special variation on the double pivot turn with cross chasse. Halfway through it I felt a firm tap on my right elbow and Amby took over. I joined Dougie at the wailing wall.

"Well?"

"She can certainly dance."

"She's a honey", Dougie enthused. "A honey."

The quickstep ended and Amby came over. There was an unfamiliar, faraway look in his eyes.

"How's Casanova?" Dougie wanted to know.

"Yon's a nice lass", Amby said, and it was more than I had ever heard him say of any female. I was impressed.

For the rest of the evening I watched the growing rivalry between my two friends. The beginning of every dance was the signal for a race across the floor towards the corner where Jean sat talking to a girl friend. Fortunes fluctuated, but on the average honours were even. At every opportunity each would cut in on the other. Dougie was enjoying himself immensely. His round face was more than usually flushed, his flaming hair more disobedient than ever. He kept dropping snippets of information:

"Her name's Jean MacDonald. She lives up the Bellbrae Road. About twenty-two. Her old man's in the Ministry of Works. She's a honey. Plays tennis."

Amby was silent. When Dougie was on the floor he watched closely, and there was a tenseness about him that I didn't like. Amby was no dancer, wasn't fond of it, yet here he was facing up to tangos, rhumbas, slow foxtrots, the whole gamut. He danced with a determined intensity that could have been amusing. But when I saw the way he looked when Dougie was up with Jean, I wasn't amused. It was a relief to me when the dance was over and we bundled into Dougie's car. They had both offered to take Jean home but she excused herself on the ground that her father was calling for her.

All the way uptown Dougie rattled on about what a honey she was, and what a dancer she was, and what he had said to her, and what she had said to him. Amby sat and said nothing. At St Mary Street we pulled up and Dougie said, "Your stop, Amby."

Amby climbed out and slammed the door. Then he poked his head in through the window and addressed Dougie in his slow, careful way. "I'd advise you to keep your filthy tongue off Miss MacDonald." Having delivered himself thus, he straightened up, turned and walked deliberately down the street towards his shop.

A minute or two passed before the amazed Dougie found any words.

"Well I'm damned! What do you suppose is wrong with him?"

"I fancy Amby has fallen in love."

"Good God!" Dougie was incredulous. "I thought he was married to his shortbread."

"Evidently it's not enough." I lit a cigarette and handed over the packet. "Come on, let's go home."

Dougie let in the clutch and, as we moved off, he shook his head and repeated, "Good God!"

These incidents were pushed to the back of my mind by a sudden and fascinating series of events concerning my own career and indeed I might have forgotten them altogether had I not met Jean MacDonald on the bus coming home from Glasgow one night two months after the fateful dance. She sat down beside me and opened the conversation.

"You're Bill Lawson, aren't you?"

"And you're Jean MacDonald. I nearly had a dance with you once."

Her smile was fleeting. "Douglas has told me about you."

"Been seeing much of Dougie, Douglas?"

"Oh yes, quite a lot. In fact, that's why I wanted to speak to you. I feel a bit guilty."

"Guilty?"

"I mean, I seem to be splitting a beautiful friendship."

"Don't let that worry you", I laughed. "I'm sure Dougie has room for both of us in that big warm heart of his."

"It's not that." She looked troubled. "It's your other friend, Amby." Her dark eyes turned on me. "I've heard of the Inseparable Three. Maybe you could do something. He frightens me."

I was reassuring. "There's no harm in Amby. He's a bit short on the social graces, that's all."

She was silent for a minute as though trying to make up her mind to something. When she did speak, it was with reluctance. "I don't want to abuse a confidence, but I feel you are the one to know what to do. You see, I went out with Amby a few times. I liked him at first. He was quiet and kind of shy. He told me about his work." She paused uncertainly.

I tried to help her. "Amby lives for his work. In his own way, he's an artist."

She struggled on. "Then he wrote me a letter. It was a pathetic letter. He asked me to marry him. I didn't know what to say, but in the end I had to write and decline his offer. It was all terribly formal. Then he wrote to Douglas a threatening letter full of queer, old-fashioned curses. Douglas laughed it off, but there was something horrible about it. It frightened me."

She stopped and smiled nervously. I was shaken. I remembered Amby on the night of the dance, the tension of him, and the venom of his parting words. At length I asked her. "Does Dougie know of your letter?"

"No", she said. "And I wouldn't have told you, only, I thought, as a friend of both of them, you could perhaps do something."

I forced a smile. "Think no more of it. I'll see what I can do."

She seemed relieved, which was more than I was. I felt uneasy. It had something to do with the strangeness of Amby. I sensed that neither Dougie nor I had ever really known him. We had grown used to his ways, had accepted him, but there was a thick crust to Amby we had never penetrated, had never tried hard enough to penetrate. I said good-night to Jean at the Cross and turned towards St Mary Street. What I should say to Amby I didn't know, but there seemed no harm in dropping in to see how he was getting on.

The window above the shop showed a light. I went through the close, up the outside stair at the back, and knocked the door. A chair scraped and there was the sound of movement inside the house, but several minutes went by before the door opened and Amby peered out into the dark landing.

"Hello, Amby. Happened to be passing. Thought I'd drop in."

The light was behind him, his face in shadow. He hesitated and I sensed his annoyance. At last he said, "Oh, it's you. Come in."

I passed him and went through the short lobby into the room. It hadn't changed since my last visit. The recessed bed was hidden by dark red velvet curtains that trailed the floor. Opposite stood the high monstrosity of wardrobe in blackening mahogany, and at the window, a sink and a gas cooker. Against the wall by the fireplace was the glass-fronted bookcase, large and ornate, which I knew to be stuffed with the queerest of old tomes. An oblong table covered by a bottle-green cloth occupied the centre of the floor and lorded it over an ill-assorted collection of dining-room chairs. There was one easy chair at the hearth. The fire was unlit but the room was stiflingly hot and smelt of baking. Nodding in the direction of the cooker, I asked, "Starting baking up here now?"

Amby grunted unintelligibly and I turned and looked at him across the table. His appearance shocked me. He had the growth of several days on his chin and his face looked pinched and drawn. His eyes, narrowed and red-rimmed, showed lines of strain at the corners. His hair was uncombed and stood up in short, black spikes all over his head. The whole of him suggested he had not washed or slept for a week.

"You look ghastly, Amby", I said. "Been overworking?"

"I haven't been working", he answered slowly in a voice that was thick and throaty like a Jake-drinker's. "The shop's been shut these two days."

I tried heavily to be jovial. "You old reprobate. Been on a bend? Why wasn't I invited?" He didn't answer and I saw his eyes flick momentarily towards the cooker. "Your cakes are burning, Amby. You'd better rescue them." He made no movement, but stared at me with eyes that held a red flame. I felt a sudden panic. He looked mad, and he looked dangerous. Without warning he leaned forward, gripped the edge of the table and spoke with a terrifying intensity.

"So he's sent you to spy on me."

I saw the knuckles whiten under the pressure of his grip and the veins stand out through the thick, black hair on the back of his hands.

"Nobody's spying on you, Amby. You're imagining things."

He waved my words aside. "You can tell Mister Dougie McVicar from me that he's not going to get her. She's a sight too good for him."

"That's unreasonable, Amby."

"Unreasonable!" He spat the word out. Then an almost tender look came into his eyes. "I never thought of a woman before the way I thought of her. It was always just my work. The shortbread. Then when I met her I knew she was just what I'd been working for all those years. I had an honest man's love for her. I'd have slaved for her." He straightened, and the wild light returned. "He poisoned her mind against me. She listened to him. And all he wanted was a night's fun, a night's fun." He made a sound almost like a sob, recovered himself, looked at me across the table and stuck out a quivering finger.

"You can warn him, as I've warned him already. The black curse is on him. He'll die the worst of deaths." He shambled over to the cooker muttering to himself as though I was no longer in the room. He threw open the oven door, and with a cloth over his hands pulled out a baking tray which he placed on the draining board.

On the tray I could see a row of little shortbread figures. I looked more closely. Each was the figure of a man in dungarees, each had a chubby face and prominent ears and an unruly coif of hair over the forehead. The rough likeness was uncanny. They were Dougie to the life. And out of each one protruded the heads of a number of large plain pins.

"What in God's name have you been doing?" I cried. But even

as I spoke I knew with sickening certainty what he had been doing. Behind me loomed the Gothic bulk of that bookcase with its library of witchcraft and black magic.

I gazed at him, horrified. He was gloating over his little figures. I had ceased to exist. I tried to think of something relevant to say. Nothing came. The room was stifling. I needed air and time to think, so I walked to the lobby, turned and said, "Good-night, Amby." He didn't look round. I don't believe he heard me. I opened the door and went out.

Next morning I rose without having reached a solution to the problem that had kept me awake most of the night. The only thing I could think of was to go round to Amby in the cold light of day. I had to convince him that this black magic rubbish was going to hurt nobody but himself. I had to convince him, but a sleepless night and the fantastic events of the evening before had left their depression. I had a foreboding. After a hurried breakfast, I set off for St Mary Street.

The shop had a deserted and forlorn air when I arrived. I climbed the dark back stair and knocked the door. There was no answer. I knocked again. I could see by the fanlight that the light was on in the house. Surely he wouldn't be sleeping with the light on. Acting on impulse, I grasped the transom, hoisted myself up and looked through the glass. What I saw made me drop quickly to the landing and attack the door. The old check lock yielded to my foot and within seconds I was bending over Amby's still figure on the floor.

He was quite dead, his face grey above the dark stubble, his mouth wide. The neck of his shirt was torn apart and his fingers were locked on the cloth. His limbs were twisted grotesquely under him. Amby had died fighting for air, in agony.

I looked round the room. Except for a chair lying on its side everything appeared to be as it had been last night. On the table lay four little shortbread men and several pieces of a fifth. The pins had been taken out and lay scattered on the table cover. I lifted one of the figures and absently broke it between my fingers. Embedded in its head, invisible from the outside, lay a large plain pin.

Methodically I collected the figures and the pins and put them in my pocket. I left only the innocent-looking pieces of shortbread. I had a last, slow look round the room and went out to find a policeman.